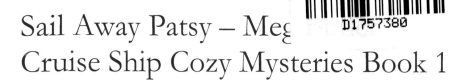

Sail Away Patsy – Meg Cruise Ship Cozy Mysteries Book 1

By Leena Clover

First Published – April 4, 2023

Chapter 1

She was nothing like the Titanic, which was a big relief. The Silver Queen resembled a modern skyscraper, her mighty decks towering over the crowded pier. I got a crick in my neck just looking up at her. Tiny figures dotted the top deck, basking in the bright sunlight. They must have boarded really early, I thought.

The long line snaking ahead of me appeared a mile long. I let out a deep sigh and smiled at the older couple before me. They were easily over seventy but they held hands. The woman had blushed when she told me they were celebrating their fiftieth anniversary. I nodded and congratulated them sincerely, sure I had made the right choice. I didn't want to wait until I was seventy to visit Alaska. Or Antarctica for that matter. I was going to spend the whole summer on the Silver Queen, working as an intern. This was just the first step toward my dream of traveling the world, visiting thirty countries before I was thirty.

My name is Meg Butler. I'm a 22 year old college student from California. Actually, I was born in the

Midwest and given up for adoption at birth but that's a story for another time. I took a gap year after high school and went on a quest to locate my birth mother. It was the best decision I made in my young life because it reunited me with three generations of my biological family, my mom Cassie, my grandma Anna and my Nonna. Quite a windfall for a lonely kid who was shuffled from one foster family to another like a hot potato.

The toddler behind me began stomping his feet and let out a wail. His father pulled him up and placed him on his shoulders.

"How much longer?" the woman beside him grumbled as the baby on her hip began to fuss. "The kids are hungry."

The man asked why she hadn't packed any snacks. She rooted around in the giant tote she was carrying and pulled out a cereal bar.

Amateurs, I smirked. My grandma had made sure I had a good breakfast before I left the hotel. A little too good, I thought now. The stack of pancakes sat heavy in my stomach and the salty bacon had left a metallic tang in my mouth. At least I don't suffer from sea sickness. I was on a week long cruise to

Mexico last winter so I considered myself a seasoned cruiser. The Silver Queen looked similar to the ship I had been on and I wasn't worried.

A server bearing a tray of glasses appeared in the distance. I licked my parched lips and leaned forward in anticipation, eager to quench my thirst with a frosty drink. The tray emptied in the fraction of a second and he turned back. Thankfully, a few more servers appeared and walked down the line toward me.

I clutched the icy cup of lemonade like a lifeline and thanked the tall, brown eyed young man in the ship's uniform. He gave a deep bow and asked if I needed anything else.

"How much longer, do you think?" I drained the tart and sweet drink and set it down, hesitating before picking up one more. "The line hasn't moved at all in the past hour."

"My apologies!" He placed a hand on his heart and looked genuinely contrite. "Royal Club members always board first." His brows furrowed. "You're not one of our Royals, are you?"

I summoned my sexiest smile and placed a hand on

my hip, jutting it out and angling my body a bit. It was a power pose that always worked for my mother.

"I could be." I wiggled my eyebrows for good measure, in case he wasn't the brightest bulb in the box.

He wanted to see the special tag I was supposed to have received in the mail.

"Never mind." I flashed a sweet smile to show there were no hard feelings. "Your job's on the line."

The woman behind me cleared her throat, surging forward to grab a drink from the tray. The guy mouthed an apology and moved down the line. The couple before me seemed unfazed, busy pouring over a guidebook. My feet were beginning to ache, thanks to the four inch stilettos I had chosen to wear that morning, a generous gift from my mother. She told me there was never a bad time to wear Manolo Blahniks. I wanted to tell her she was wrong, very wrong.

I saw the Adonis turn back and walk toward me with an empty tray. I grabbed his sleeve. "Isn't there any way to speed this up?"

He apologized profusely. "I'll see what I can do."

Half an hour later, there was no sign of him but the line had mercifully moved forward. I finally set foot on the ramp leading up to the welcome area on board, accepting a glass of bubbly from a girl who was about my age. A dapper man in a pastel suit introduced himself as the cruise director and told me they were running late.

"Why don't you head to the grand buffet for a spot of lunch?" He put a hand on my back and gently guided me in the right direction. "We set sail at 1900 hours. There's a party on the top deck later."

"Oh, the Sail Away party?" I beamed. "No way I'm gonna miss it."

I had handed over my documents to a squat, square jawed man at the check-in kiosk. He gave them back to me, his eyes full of regret.

"I'm sorry but you are not on the list, Miss."

The cruise director didn't bat an eyelid, his avuncular manner unruffled.

"Are you sure you're on the right ship, my dear?"

It was a valid question because two more Alaska bound ships were in dock and were being boarded at the same time. But I didn't make errors like this.

I tried to curb the indignation that rose in my throat, irked by his patronizing manner. The anniversary couple were posing for a photo under a big sign proclaiming the ship's name.

"This is the Silver Queen, isn't it?" I exhaled. "My name is Meg Butler and this is where I'm supposed to be, on a cruise to Alaska."

The cruise director asked for my cabin number.

"I don't have one." I was patient. "They said I would be allotted a room once I reported for duty."

His eyes twinkled with mirth and a dimple appeared in his left cheek. This guy seemed to get off on making fun of people.

A stout woman with a heaving bosom materialized out of nowhere and grabbed my arm in a tight grip. I felt myself being pulled away from the reception area. Before I realized what was happening, I had been packed into an elevator that plunged downwards into the depths of the ship.

"Excuse me!" I tried to wrench my arm free. "You have no right to manhandle me like this."

"Shut up!" the woman hissed in my ear.

The elevator doors opened and the woman took me down a long corridor that seemed to stretch forever. After what seemed like a mile but was probably just a hundred feet, she pushed open a door marked Training Manager and dumped me on a metal chair.

"Tell me your name again."

"Meg Butler. I'm an intern on this ship." I sprang to my feet, rubbing my sore arm. "I demand to know who you are, Madam. I'm going to report you to the captain."

The woman's cackle chilled my bones. She could easily star in a horror movie.

"You will do no such thing, Meg Butler. You realize I could throw you off this vessel right now?"

"But what have I done?" I didn't hold back my outrage.

My life has taught me to stand up for my rights. People will bully you if you let them. It doesn't hurt to set the ground rules from the beginning.

"You were supposed to be here at five, girl." She

banged a fist on the table. "That's when the other interns got here."

I glanced at my watch. It showed thirty minutes past three so I was early.

"Not 5 PM!" The woman rolled her eyes. "5 AM! You are almost twelve hours late."

Who reports to work at five in the morning? My confidence began to slip. Had I committed a blunder on day one?

"And are you wearing heels?" she clucked, shaking her head in disbelief. "They will have to go, of course." She eyed the phone in my hand. "You will have to turn that in too."

"What?" My palms were beginning to sweat. "The induction manual didn't say anything about that."

I had promised Grandma I would call her every day at 6 PM California time. She was bound to panic if she couldn't get in touch with me. There was no telling what my extended family would do if they thought I was in danger.

"I'm the boss here, girl, in case you haven't realized. All the interns report to me and so will you. My word is law. You better get that straight or get off this ship right now."

Leaving the ship wasn't an option. I had turned down a summer in Tuscany to be an intern on the Silver Queen. My friend Barry called in a big favor to get me into this much coveted program. Grandma and her friends had thrown a big party in my honor, just before I left Dolphin Bay. There was no way I was going to walk down that gangway with my tail between my legs.

"I can be so stupid." I stared down at my feet and apologized for being late. "Please don't send me away. I've been looking forward to this trip for weeks."

"You're not a tourist," she corrected me primly. "You are here to work. I will not say this again."

I assured her I wasn't afraid of hard work, bringing up the many hours I had labored in my grandma's café.

"You won't just be pouring coffee," my formidable boss lady warned. "Although you will do a few shifts in the café and the main dining room. My interns get a taste of every department on the ship. This helps them choose a specific position when they apply for a full time job."

"That's great. I'm here to learn." I had been trying to read the name off the tag she wore. I finally pieced the letters together. "R K Powell. What does R K stand for?"

"Here's a piece of free advice." Her smile made me shiver. "Keep your head down, do what you are told and don't speak unless you're spoken to."

I pressed my lips together and gave her a thumbs up. She didn't crack a smile. Clearly, this woman had a giant piece of driftwood lodged somewhere on her person. I had dealt with her kind before and I told myself I could do it again. It was a small price to pay for spending the next three months in Alaska.

R K Powell marched down the corridor, signaling me to follow her. This time we walked several hundred feet before she stopped suddenly and pushed open a door to reveal a closet sized space. I spotted two bunks against a wall and a tiny nightstand with some shelves. My eyes widened in horror as a creeping suspicion entered my mind.

"This is your cabin." RK swept an arm around. "You

will share it with another girl. Looks like she had a choice of bunks because she was here on time."

No balcony then, I muttered to myself. Not even a port hole. A loud hum filled the air around us, making it impossible to think.

"What's that noise?" I spoke without thinking.

"Those are the engines," R K Powell replied. "They are just warming them up."

My boss opened another cabinet and ran a finger down the contents.

"Two sets of uniform and a set of sensible shoes. They better be spotless at all times. You do your own laundry, okay?"

She was meeting all the interns on the top deck in ten minutes and expected me to be there. I started flinging off my clothes as soon as she stepped out of the room. I howled in pain as my elbow hit the wall beside me and a bottle of body lotion burst open, emptying its contents on the new dress I had worn to make a good first impression. I was stuck in a tiny space barely large enough to stretch my arms in.

How was I going to survive the next three months aboard the Silver Queen?

Chapter 2

The elevator finally landed on the top deck and I waited until the mass of people streamed out. It had taken forever, stopping at almost every floor, using up the ten minutes the RK monster had allotted me.

The deck was crammed with guests and the atmosphere was festive. Balloons and streamers proudly proclaimed the party was on, so did a big sign announcing the Sail Away party. People lined the railing, bagging coveted spots so they could wave at the crowd on the pier.

The band was playing a catchy tune and my feet picked up the beat. I gravitated toward the stage, looking around for any sign of my boss. The uniform she had provided was a few sizes too large and made me look like a scarecrow. I needed something that suited my petite frame.

"Are you taking requests?" I asked the drummer and hailed a girl carrying a tray of drinks. "Weren't you serving bubbly in the welcome area?" I thought the smile I greeted her with was friendly enough.

Her blue eyes clouded with worry, growing wide as her neck jerked to one side.

"Come with me," she muttered. "Now!"

I stared at her back, dumbstruck, then hurried after her. She went behind a screen and led me to a table loaded with an array of colorful drinks. An Asian boy hefted a gallon sized pitcher, carefully pouring it into empty glasses. The Adonis I'd spotted on the pier loaded a tray and turned around, his mouth settling in a smirk when he spotted me.

"Hello again!" I gave him a finger wave. "I finally boarded."

He ignored me completely and stalked off.

"What's with him?" I wondered out loud.

"That's Mickey!" the blue eyed girl sighed. "He's just sucking up to the boss." She put a hand on my shoulder and peered into my eyes. "Look, are you serious about this internship? You didn't report on time this morning so you missed orientation. And you're late again! RK's not happy."

The Asian boy had been listening in.

"I think you should get off the boat before we lift anchor."

I didn't know why all these people were trying to discourage me. My eyes narrowed and my mouth set in the mulish expression that's just like my mother's.

"Do you know how hard I worked to land this internship? No way I'm giving up now." I sucked in a breath. "What's your problem, anyway? Did they hire you to haze new interns?"

The girl grew exasperated.

"We're interns too. And we're just trying to help you, Meg."

"You know my name?"

"Of course!" the boy snorted. "You're infamous, girl. There's a crew pool about how many hours you'll last. The current odds are seventeen to one."

This was getting out of hand.

"Bet on me," I advised. "You'll make a bundle. Meg Butler never pulls back from a challenge."

Blue eyes drew closer.

"Forget all that. RK's coming this way. Just load a tray of drinks and start serving the guests, Meg. We'll all be in trouble if a single guest complains."

There's a time to stick to your guns but this wasn't it. I had to choose my battles if I wanted to survive this internship. So I picked up the tray the Asian boy slid toward me and joined the milieu. Before I knew what was happening, the tray of drinks flew from my hands and the floor rushed to meet me. A pair of fleshy arms caught me just in time.

"Are you alright?" A short, rotund man with a bald pate and a gigantic belly hanging over a thick leather belt asked me.

I thanked him and looked around, my cheeks burning with shame. My gaze landed on the Adonis, or Mickey as the girl had called him. He gave me an obsequious bow but made no move to help. I wasn't fooled for a minute. I had seen him from the corner of my eye just a fraction of a second before I went airborne.

"You tripped me on purpose."

His eyebrows shot up, his mouth hanging open in shock. Mickey had definitely taken drama lessons.

I felt a familiar vice like grip on my arm again and a voice breathed fire in my ear. Flinching at the sudden waft of ketchup and mustard, I allowed myself to be dragged toward the screen, just as the blue eyed girl from before arrived with a mop to clean up my mess.

"When do we eat?" I burst out as my stomach gave a low growl. "Breakfast was a long time ago."

RK didn't bother to reply. She pointed at the bartender and a line of pitchers standing guard on the drinks table. Apparently, she couldn't risk letting me loose among the passengers. I was to be relegated to pouring the drinks, out of sight of any poor, hapless passenger who might cross my path.

"Can you manage this?" she asked. "Can you pour these drinks into these glasses without hurting anyone?"

I bristled at the insult. My resume clearly stated I had worked at a café for the past couple of years.

"Easy peasy," I assured her. "Chill, okay?"

The RK monster curled her fists and turned her back on me. Her temper was going to be an issue for her. But I was wise enough to know she wouldn't care for my opinion.

I picked up a pitcher and started filling the glasses

one by one, faint with hunger. The last two years in Dolphin Bay had spoiled me. My body was used to being fed every two or three hours, given to overindulgence. Gone was the time when I could thrive on watery soup and a piece of stale bread for days.

"Can you spare a couple of olives?" I begged the bartender. "I'm dying with hunger."

He took pity on me and conjured a tray of canapés from an unseen shelf. I wasn't going to look a gift horse in the mouth. Setting the pitcher down, I stuffed two crab puffs in my mouth at once, barely hearing his warning about washing my hands. Two sticky chicken wings, five tiny meatballs and what seemed like a dozen cucumber sandwiches later, I finally came up for air. The food was tasty so the kitchen on the ship wasn't a problem. I just had to get past the sentries or find a kind soul to feed me.

The bartender had finished mixing two more pitchers. He nudged me toward a sanitizer dispenser mounted on the wall. I doused my hands liberally, gulping fresh air to avoid the alcohol fumes. Mickey materialized and started stacking a tray.

"Let me do that for you." I extended an olive branch.

Kitchen staff arrived with a trolley of more canapés. Mickey clapped one of them on the back and a silent message passed between them. He stooped down to pick up a tiny plate of canapés from the bottom, covered with a cloth.

"The chicken wings are dope," I told Mickey. "Why don't you take a break while I load these trays?"

I can be quick when I want to but I hadn't anticipated the warp speed at which Mickey could gobble his food. He was back at my elbow just when I squeezed the final glass onto his tray. RK arrived at the same instant.

"How's she doing, Mickey?" she asked. "Can she be trusted with the drinks?"

I sensed he was going to throw me under the bus.

"I was about to taste one of these drinks, Ma'am." He picked up a blue drink from the tray and handed it to her. "Would you like to do the honors?"

"Better safe than sorry, huh?" RK approved the suggestion and accepted the drink. "You try the pink martini."

Mickey obliged her with a bow, picked up the glass

and took a deep swallow along with RK. I didn't get any warning. Twin streams of pink and blue spewed out of their mouths, hitting me in the face. Icy rivulets trickled down my chest and back, staining my uniform. Who was going to foot my dry cleaning bill?

"What have you done?" The RK monster shrieked.

A string of expletives followed.

"Do you want to poison the passengers?"

Her hand shook as she dabbed a finger on my chest.

"That's it. Get off this ship right now. You're an accident waiting to happen. The captain will have my job if something happens to the passengers."

I picked up a glass from the tray and proceeded to drain it. Had the bartender watered them down or made them too strong?

It was RK's turn to get sprayed.

"This is vile!" I spluttered. "Where did you hire that bartender?"

The man in question had been observing us, deftly mixing more drinks like an automaton. He finally set the cocktail shaker down and came over to see what the problem was.

"Nico here has been a bartender for ten years," RK stormed. "Ten years on this ship and he's never mixed a wrong drink."

The bartender's dark eyes flitted between us.

"Too strong?" he frowned. "I follow recipe."

"More like too soapy," I told him, placing a hand on my hip. "Why did you put detergent in the drinks?"

His eyebrows shot up, his eyes growing wide in alarm.

"This is all your fault," RK screeched. "You've got some nerve, blaming this poor man. Did you think you could pull some silly college prank here?"

Mickey had been quiet all this time, standing with arms folded in front of him, head down. He suddenly sprang to life.

"Why don't we search her?"

RK was skeptical.

"She can't be that dumb …"

Mickey told her there was no harm in looking. She could send me home if she found evidence of foul play.

The blue eyed girl arrived just then with an empty tray, followed by the cute Asian guy. RK ordered her to search me.

I protested. Did she think I was some kind of convict?

"Do you want me to call security?" The RK monster threatened.

I was sure she was bluffing. The Sail Away party was in full swing. The ship had sailed while I had been pouring the five hundred and ninety three drinks. The twinkling lights of shore were barely visible in the distance. Would RK really risk breaking up the party? The passengers came first, after all.

"No need." I shook my head. "And you won't even have to apologize when you're proven wrong."

RK gave a nod and Blue Eyes started patting my

pockets, mumbling an apology only I could hear. Her hand stilled as something rustled in my pants.

"What was that?" RK asked sharply.

She lunged forward to thrust a hand in my pocket.

"Wait a minute," I protested, doing the honors myself, pulling out an empty plastic sachet.

I stared in horror at the object I held. Nobody could mistake the familiar red packet of detergent. My mind stopped working when I needed it the most.

RK was breathing fire. Mickey looked like the cat that ate the canary. The blue eyed girl was petrified and the cute guy cowered behind her.

"Troublemaker!" My boss could barely breathe. "Get outta my sight. Now!"

Her temper was justified this time because I had been caught red handed. At least she believed so. But I had to say something in my defense.

"I'm innocent."

RK grabbed my arm again and almost pushed me toward the elevator. The last thing I saw when the doors closed was my fellow intern

Mickey, drawing a finger across his throat, his mouth curled in a sinister smile.

Chapter 3

Loud music blared through hidden speakers, beating louder than my heart. Slick bodies splashed in the pool, the more child like indulging in cannon balls that drenched the rest of us every minute. The crew of the Silver Queen sure knew how to party. But was I still one of them?

Being banished to my room hadn't crushed my spirits. I lay down on the bottom bunk, mentally daring my unseen roommate to object. Sleep came easily and I must have napped for an hour or two. The engines gave a violent shudder, waking me up. I sat up suddenly and banged my head against the top bunk. Don't judge me, but I panicked. What if there was a gash in my head? Who was going to take me to the emergency room? Then I realized I was on a floating bucket with no hospital in sight.

It was a while before I talked myself into taking deep breaths. Had the sentry outside the door heard me? Why wasn't he rushing in to help? I pulled the door open and looked up and down the long corridor. A couple of show girls hurried down and pushed open a door. A man dressed as a waiter shuffled along, yawning his head off and disappeared behind another door. None of them spared me a second glance.

There was no guard on my door and nobody was keeping tabs on me.

The early bird gets the worm. So does the quick one. I wasn't about to waste this golden opportunity. I rushed back into my cabin and squeezed myself into the tiny bathroom, looking for a medicine cabinet. The mirror showed I wasn't the worse for wear. Splashing some cold water on my face, I finger combed my shoulder length hair and smoothed my hands down the soiled uniform. Better get changed, I thought. I was all set to explore the ship, before anyone returned with my marching orders.

The elevator began to fill up after Deck 2. Most people were going to the buffet to grab a snack before taking in a show. I followed the crowd and found myself in a giant dining area with a few dozen buffet stations. In the interest of keeping it simple, I grabbed two slices of pepperoni pizza and bagged a table for two behind a ficus. The bout of homesickness hit out of nowhere. I teared up and tried to swallow the big cheesy bite I had taken, thinking of my mom and my grandma. They were going to drive back to Dolphin Bay the next morning. Maybe I would beat them home. Would the cruise ship spring for a plane ticket for a disgraced intern?

I finished the pizza, feeling sorry for myself. Life had forced me to be street smart at an early age but here I was, in the doghouse because of a major faux pas. I'm referring to the mix up about the reporting time, not the detergent laced drinks. That had been a nasty prank and someone had thought I was gullible enough to be framed for it. Clearly, the past few years in Dolphin Bay had dulled my instincts and made me appear like a pampered princess. It was time to set the record straight.

The corridor was deserted when I got back and the cabin was empty. I climbed up to the top bunk this time and sat cross legged, waiting for the RK monster to arrive with my sentence. The door flung open after ten minutes or twenty. It was hard to keep track of time in that tiny closet.

The blue eyed girl who had been serving drinks rushed in and began pulling clothes out of a tiny drawer.

"Get dressed." She pulled her tee shirt above her head. "Party on Deck 1."

I looked away as she undressed completely and pulled on a bikini. Then she stepped into a glittering dress that barely reached her thigh.

"RK might come looking for me."

"It's midnight, way past the RK monster's bed time."

"You call her that too?" I jumped down from the bunk.

"What else?" Blue Eyes grinned. "She deserves it."

I thrust a hand forward, deciding it was time to introduce myself.

"I'm Meg."

She pulled me close and wrapped her arms around me.

"Ashley Dodge. You can call me Ash."

She held me by the arms and narrowed her eyes.

"Do you have any party clothes?"

I told her I hadn't unpacked yet. There was no point if I was to be sent back home.

"Just borrow something of mine then." She wrinkled her nose and waved a hand at the tiny set of drawers. "We're the same size."

We both burst out laughing.

"Yeah," I nodded. "Except, you're like a foot taller."

Ashley took my hand and led me down the long endless corridor.

"This is the I-95," she told me. "It runs along the length of the ship."

I had never been east of Ohio so I had only heard of the highway that stretched across the east coast of the United States.

We stepped behind another unmarked door and climbed up two flights of a metal staircase to Deck 1. Ashley told me some of the officers and staff had cabins on it.

"The lucky ones like the entertainers and speakers, you know?"

I wondered what we were doing there. I didn't have to wait long to find out. The blast of cold air was unexpected. It was like stepping into a freezer after being cooped up in my tiny closet sized quarters.

"You'll warm up soon enough," Ashley promised.

Throngs of people surrounded a modest pool, made up of a variety of ethnicities and nationalities. My friend Barry had told me about the crew on a cruise ship. Apparently, the conditions were so harsh and the pay so poor that only people from third world countries could make a living out of it. North Americans generally steered clear.

The throng parted as Ashley approached, still holding my hand. She introduced me to a number of people who smiled and nodded and patted me on the back. Someone thrust a bottle of beer in my hand.

"Where are we?" I screamed in Ashley's ear, trying to be heard above the noise.

"Crew deck." She started swaying in tune to the music, urging me to join her. "Isn't it dope? They party like this every night."

"Have you been on this ship before?" I wondered how she knew so many people. "Are they all interns?"

"Oh, no, Meg! There's just four of us. I'll introduce you in a minute."

She hailed a dark haired guy with large eyes and a come hither expression.

"This is Luca. He works in the kitchen."

He put an arm around her waist and pulled her into a jig. I gathered Ashley hadn't wasted any time snagging a bae, or beau, as my grandma would say.

After a dozen more introductions, my head was reeling with all the strange names.

"Come and meet the interns."

Ashley took my hand again and we plunged further in the crowd, heading toward the deck railing. Two guys stood there, watching the revelry, their eyes gleaming with excitement.

"You know Mickey." Ashley nodded at the tall Adonis I had encountered before.

He gave the ridiculous deep bow again and properly introduced himself.

"Mickey Singh from Queens. Nice to meet you, Meg Butler."

I gave him the cold shoulder and turned to the cute Asian guy. He was my height and eager to please.

"Kim Jeong Soo." He pumped my hand vigorously.

"Hello Meg!"

"Hi Kim," I smiled back. "Where are you from?"

He explained Kim was his family name.

"Call me Jeong Soo," he urged. "I'm from California too, from the Bay Area."

I immediately wanted to know which university he went to.

"UC Santa Barbara?" I hazarded a guess.

He was going to Berkley next year but was hoping to get into Harvard or Yale. Ashley ruffled his hair and told me he was still in high school.

"He's a minor, our very own Doogie Houser."

Jeong Soo blushed and told me Ashley was right. He hoped to be a doctor one day.

"So why are you working on a cruise ship?" I quizzed.

"Just to get something unique on my resume," he explained. "Ivy League schools are looking for that."

Jeong Soo hoped to put in some extra time at the ship's medical center.

"What about you, Meg?"

I told them I hoped to do a stint on a cruise ship once I graduated from college.

"I'm going to visit thirty countries before I'm thirty," I informed them, ignoring Mickey's smirk. "Working on a cruise ship gives me the best of both worlds. I get paid to travel across the world."

"Provided you can keep a job for 24 hours," Mickey howled. "You make me crack up."

Ashley didn't volunteer any information about herself.

"Come on, Mickey. We interns need to stick together. There's just four of us."

"Oh, no, sista!" Mickey wasn't having any of it. "It's every man for himself. And it's just you, me and the kid here after RK chucks Meg out on her hiney tomorrow.

"What do you have against me?" I smiled at Mickey. "Or does bullying come naturally to you?"

"I like you," he replied. "We could get along like a house on fire in another place and time. But you're in my way now."

Ashley explained his cryptic statement.

"He wants to win the prize."

"What prize?" I realized how clueless I sounded the moment the words left my mouth. "I mean, doesn't everyone?"

"I don't," Jeong Soo shrugged. "So it's the best of three, really."

"Winning the internship prize means a glowing recommendation from the RK monster." Ashley sounded hushed. "That will get you a job on any cruise line in the world."

"And a guaranteed position right here on the Silver Queen," Mickey added. "So excuse me if I want to win."

Actually, I still had a couple of years of college to finish. My family and I were on the same page on this point. I wasn't going to start a full time job until I graduated. So technically, Ashley was Mickey's only adversary. But I wasn't going to tell him that.

"Afraid of a little competition?" I needled.

"I never underestimate anyone." Mickey dug his arms in the pockets of his cargo shorts. "But you dug your own grave, sweetheart."

I realized he was probably right. My fate would be revealed with the rising sun. Until then, I was a young girl on a ship bound for Alaska with a wild party raging around me. The night was young and I wasn't going to waste a single minute of it.

Chapter 4

I floated in the water on my surf board, eyeing the wave rushing toward me. It was a big one. In a fraction of a second, I performed a delicate maneuver and stood up on the board, knees bent. Then I was soaring across the water, my arms stretched wide, the sun warming my back. Mom and Grandma waved at me from Paradise Beach. Someone shook me violently and I went under, kicking my legs to reach the surface.

The dream was pleasant while it lasted.

"Wake up, Meg!" Ashley screamed in my ear. "The RK monster wants to see you in her office in ten minutes."

I sat up with a jerk, once again banging my head against the roof of the cabin. At this rate, my forehead would be studded with bumps of various shapes and sizes. I could have a whole mountain range as my crown.

"It's show time, then." I jumped down and grabbed the clothes Ashley was holding out and made a beeline for the bathroom.

"Just do it here," she groaned. "I'll close my eyes."

I am really not comfortable with undressing before strangers. Although Ashley acted like my long lost sibling and didn't hold back, I was a bit cautious about getting too close. But the clock was ticking so I turned around and hastily pulled on the jeans and shirt. I felt a tug at my hair and realized Ashley had volunteered to brush the tangles out of my hair.

"Go, Go, Go!" she pushed me out of the door, slipping me a breath mint.

I ran a dozen steps before realizing I didn't know where I was going. Ashley read my mind.

"It's that black door marked Training Manager."

Several people passed me as I hurtled toward my destination. Common sense told me it must be morning but I still had no idea of the time.

RK Powell crooked a finger and ordered me to sit without saying a single word. I braced myself. I was already prepared for the worst and had mentally drafted an email to the inn owners in Tuscany, begging them to reconsider having me.

"I'm willing to give you another chance, Margaret."

This was the last thing I had expected her to say. I was so shocked I didn't even correct her. Most people butcher my name, thinking Meg is short for something. I'm tired of explaining how my mother named me after Meg Ryan, her screen idol from the 90s.

"I got the reporting time wrong but I didn't mess up the drinks."

RK cut me off and continued.

"Today is a sea day. Most passengers like to spend time on deck, engaging in a variety of activities. The interns will be assigned different tasks through the day."

"I'm a people person. So …"

"You are doing housekeeping. Don't even think about slacking off."

I couldn't hide a smile. RK was all bluster if this was her idea of punishment. Running a vacuum and folding sheets was something I could handle easily.

"No worries," I assured her. "I'm not afraid of hard

work."

"I hope you realize the opportunity I'm giving you." RK puffed up.

She didn't want to own up to the top brass. Letting me go meant she had failed to handle four college kids. I barely heard her next words.

"Take this time to reflect on what this internship can do for you."

Was she going to demand a thousand word essay on the topic?

"So you're not casting me off then?" I beamed.

"Not yet." RK waved her hand to dismiss me.

I couldn't get out of there fast enough but I remembered to thank her. A voice in my head told me I had no idea where to go next. My body screamed for coffee. The crew party had raged until pink streaks of dawn kissed the horizon. I vaguely remembered following Ashley to our cabin. However many hours of sleep I had managed to get, it wasn't enough. I longed for a stack of chocolate chip pancakes, a big mug of coffee and a plush mattress, in that order. Apparently, none of them were in my immediate future.

I made haste to leave RK's cabin and ran into a wall.

"This is Edna," RK's silky voice crooned in my ear. "I have entrusted you in her care."

Edna was built like a tank and looked as approachable as a porcupine. I gulped and met her eye, trying my best not to shake like a leaf. All I got was a hard glare. She turned and lumbered down the I-95, giving me no choice but to scurry after her. The elevator spit us out on Deck 8 where I followed her into Housekeeping Central. I was put in charge of a massive cart loaded with every kind of cleaning product, handed a fresh apron and a mob cap that screamed Downton Abbey.

"I have to eat," I blurted. "You don't want me falling face down into these chemicals."

Edna opened a tiny refrigerator wedged between the wall and a massive sink and pulled out an energy bar and a bottle of chocolate milk. So she wasn't inhuman.

I thanked her profusely, earning a pat on my arm. I took a hefty bite of the bar and chugged the milk with one hand, using my other hand and body weight to push the cart out into the lobby. The bar tasted like saw dust and I marveled at the dreamer who had named it after something as decadent as carrot cake. It was fantastic at best and sadistic at worst.

We took the elevator up to Deck 11. Sunlight hit a polished wood railing at the far end and a cool breeze laced with the salty air caressed my face. Scrubbing the decks didn't seem that daunting.

Edna continued to walk down the lobby. I saw her turn around and fix her steely eyes on me.

"Coming!" I pushed the cart with all my might and almost ran her over.

She stayed the momentum of the cart with one hand and pushed open a door marked Queen's Quarters. My mouth fell open at the sight that greeted us.

"Has a twister blown through here?" I didn't feel too good all of a sudden.

Chaos reigned inside. Heavy brocade swathed furniture stood upturned. The thick Oriental carpet was littered with shards of broken glass and china, crusted with dried food. The massive ten foot TV covering a wall was cracked like a windshield. Music blared through unseen speakers at a deafening pitch.

I mutely followed in Edna's wake, dreading to see a body or two in the bedroom. Pieces of clothing covered every available surface, ripped to shreds. Some of the labels were still intact and I marveled at the designers' names.

Edna tapped me on the shoulder and pointed to the bathroom. An atrocious odor of unknown origin attacked my senses as I went closer to the door. Edna settled into the armchair next to the bed, put her feet up and started snoring.

The rest of the day was a blur. The only thing I was aware of as I pushed the cart out of the elevator on Deck 8 and followed Edna to Housekeeping Central was my soiled apron, my raw hands and the ache in my back. My arms hurt from scrubbing every inch of two thousand square feet dozens of times and my eyes stung from being exposed to industry strength cleaning products. Edna had taken pity on me and held the trash bag while I picked up the million pieces of debris.

"Good." Edna wasn't a woman of words but her eyes softened as she dismissed me with another pat on the arm.

I don't know how I found my way to the crew mess.

My eyes fell on the soft serve machine and I almost hugged it in relief. I managed to pull the handle and load a cup.

"Dude, where have you bin?" Ashley yelled from a table.

She sat really close to Luca, a slice of pizza in her hands. I salivated at the smell of the toppings and the cheese. Mickey had a bowl of noodles before him and Jeong Soo was picking at a plate of salad. I swallowed the entire cup of soft serve before I reached their table.

"Aren't you leaving tomorrow?" Mickey asked slyly. "Don't expect a farewell."

Ashley told him to shut up and slid the pizza pie toward me. I didn't need to be asked twice. I closed my eyes and didn't open them until I'd chowed down a few slices. It was surprisingly good.

"What else?" I asked.

Luca recommended the Chicken Tikka Masala. One of the British chefs made a big pan every day. Mickey thought the Korean glass noodles he was eating were delicious.

"Want," I nodded, unable to take the effort to form a whole sentence.

Ashley understood and hopped over to the buffet. She came back with two plates loaded with half a dozen different dishes from around the world.

"What does RK say?" she wanted to know. "Are you staying or leaving."

I gave a shrug and dug a fork into the glass noodles, deftly picking up some sushi with some chopsticks. Edna held my fate in her hands but I was too tired to explain.

"Tell her about our day, Ash," Jeong Soo prompted. "She can listen while she eats."

"We met a lot of guests," Ashley humored him. "But mostly we spent the day taking care of a group. It's a bunch of people from some community in Colorado."

Mickey wasn't happy with how the group had treated them.

"Then why were you buttering up that old woman? Any tips we get will be shared between the four of us. RK told us that during orientation."

"Who's to stop that hag from slipping me a 50?" Mickey quirked an eyebrow. "I massaged her smelly feet for half an hour." He darted a nasty look in my direction. "Unlike some 'interns' who were playing hooky."

I didn't have the strength to correct him.

"We're going to spend the day with them tomorrow," Jeong Soo informed us. "They signed up for the Highlights of Ketchikan tour."

"What about the three days in Anchorage?" Ashley grumbled. "Are we going to be stuck with them again?"

I wasn't aware of the Silver Queen's itinerary. All I knew was we would be making round trips to and from Alaska all summer.

"Three days in the same port?" I was puzzled. "Is that usual?"

Ashley launched into a lengthy explanation. I was beginning to rely on her.

"It's more common in Europe. People do a land portion before or after the cruise in Alaska but the Silver Queen is going to change all that."

The ship would be docked in Anchorage for three days. Passengers had a choice of taking a three day trip to Denali National Park or staying on the ship and taking a different excursion every day.

"That group's going to Denali." Ashley had heard some kids talking. "I won't mind being at their beck and call if it means we can ride the train and visit the park."

"Sounds exciting." I realized what I was going to miss out on. "Thanks for the food, Ash."

She gave me a fist bump and a brilliant smile, reading my mind again.

"Don't worry, bud. I'm sure RK won't get rid of you yet. The cruise line will have to pay a lot to send you home and the monster will have to explain why."

"She's not gonna do that," Luca nodded. "You're stuck with us, bella!"

Jeong Soo agreed with them and shook my hand vigorously. Mickey was the only one who didn't look happy.

Chapter 5

A loud banging on the door woke me up. I almost sat up but some survival instinct must have held me back. Jeong Soo pushed the door open and peeped in, eyes averted. He was beyond cute.

"Intern meeting in RK's office in 20 minutes."

Ashley groaned from under the covers and told him to go away. I thanked him and promised we'd be there.

"You don't mind if I shower first?"

I didn't expect a reply. The hot water felt good on my skin. I had wisely chosen to skip the crew party the previous night, earning a nasty look from Ashley. I hope she wasn't the type to bear grudges. I had dropped off soon as I hit the bunk, too tired to complain about how hard it was. I wrapped up my shower after banging my elbow in the wall a few times, ready to face anything. Now if only I could get a cup of coffee.

I poked Ashley a few times and left her to her own devices. The crew mess was full of new faces. Some nodded at me but most were in a hurry to report to their stations. I spotted Jeong Soo and Mickey and decided to join them.

"Did you put your luggage outside your cabin?" Mickey's voice was silky smooth. "That's what the passengers do on disembarkation day."

I was beginning to get a headache.

"Six impossible things before breakfast …" I muttered.

"What's that, eh?" He was blank.

Jeong Soo rushed to explain the literary reference.

"Could you be any more nerdy, Jeong Soo?" Mickey was harsh. "What are you even doing here?"

"I know!" Jeong Soo beamed. "I'm going to be cool by the time I finish this internship."

I shoveled some eggs and toast and refilled my coffee in record time. Mickey tapped his watch and we rushed down the I-95, not wanting to be late. Ashley joined us half way. We trooped into RK's cabin single file. I hoped I didn't have ketchup on my shirt.

"Good Morning!" RK gave us a quick once over and pointed to a white board on the wall behind her. My name was on it, or a version of it.

"The Internship Challenge officially begins today," she informed us. "I will update this leader board every day, based on your performance."

She made an example out of me.

"Margaret's name is on the bottom because she has had some …" she paused to find the right word, "misadventures, shall we say?"

I caught on immediately. A complaint from the staff or passengers would move the person down and any praise would bump them up. I didn't think there was a lot of scope for vertical movement since there were just the four of us.

After a brief lecture about our expected behavior, RK escorted us to the dining room to meet our tour group. It was 8 AM and the ship had already docked in Ketchikan, our first port of call in Alaska. I admit I was excited.

A dozen people were spread across two tables, loaded with the debris of a lavish buffet breakfast. Many of the discarded plates had barely been touched. A pre-teen boy took one bite from a plate of Eggs Benedict, made a face and pushed it away.

"Aren't you going to eat that?" I asked before RK had a chance to introduce us. "Do you know how many people in the world don't get one square meal a day?"

The kid turned red and started bawling. Maybe he was an oversized toddler.

"How dare you?" A man sitting at the opposite end of the table shot up and towered over me, his green eyes sparkling with barely suppressed anger. "That's my son."

"Waste not, want not," I preached. "You should teach him to respect food."

RK was clearing her throat loudly, trying to grab my attention. Mickey was trying hard not to laugh. Jeong Soo and Ashley looked stricken.

"My son will never want for anything," the man thundered. "I've made sure of that."

What did he know? Fate was fickle and likely to desert you in an instant. I opened my mouth to warn him but RK beat me to the punch.

"That's enough, Margaret."

She introduced us and basically told the group we were at their mercy. It was our job to take care of their slightest need. Then she explained how they were supposed to grade us at the end of the day.

"I didn't sign up for this," a brown haired man wearing a pink camp shirt squeaked.

Everyone ignored him.

"When do we get our vouchers?" the green eyed man demanded. "My wife has booked a massage this evening and we have tickets for Mamma Mia."

"All taken care of," RK assured them. "You get VIP seating for all shows, 50% off at the spa and specialty restaurants and a free upgrade to suites in Denali. And you get 40% off any new cruise you book while you're on board."

The man looked pleased. I guessed he had negotiated all those perks for letting us fetch and carry for the group.

"You are signed up for the Highlights of Ketchikan tour," RK reminded them. "It starts at 9 AM sharp. I think you should leave now."

Chairs were pushed back and last sips of coffee were

taken. A couple of women wanted to use the restroom before they left. Then everyone wanted to go. I was dispatched to get some snacks and bottled water.

There was a long line to get off the ship but the group got priority. Apparently, this was another perk they got for letting us serve them.

I filled my lungs with the fresh air and looked around, feasting on the landscape around me. The ground felt funny and I struggled to keep my balance. Ashley laughed and held my arm until the old woman asked for a drink. I pulled a bottle of juice from the heavy basket I was carrying and passed it along. She wanted sparkling water.

"We don't have any," I apologized.

This didn't go down well.

"I gave specific instructions to my room steward," she roared. "I don't drink anything other than sparkling water."

My shoulders slumped. The only way I could salvage the situation was go back to the ship and get her some. Surprisingly, the green eyed man came to my rescue.

"Can't you make do, Cecilia? We are late for the tour." He didn't wait for her reply, putting a hand on Mickey's shoulder. "Lead the way."

To my knowledge, Mickey had never been to Ketchikan before. I had no idea where to go and my guess was, Mickey didn't either. But he was smarter than I thought. He strode toward a building marked Visitor Center, recommending it as the quintessential first stop.

Ashley spotted a woman near the entrance, holding a sign for the Ketchikan Highlights Tour. She pulled me along with her, hollering at everyone to follow us.

The woman led us to another pier where a modest boat awaited us. It seemed tiny compared to the Silver Queen. A bearded man wearing a captain's hat welcomed us aboard. With a pang, I realized the entire three hour tour was to be on the boat. There went my chance to stretch my legs on land.

It was a gray day and mist shrouded the peaks around us. The water was murky and there was a chill in the air. I had taken Ashley's advice and dressed in layers so I could stand on deck to admire the picture postcard views. Half the tour group had chosen to sit at a table inside in the temperature controlled area.

Mickey had tagged along with the old woman called Cecilia and I could see him giving her a foot massage. The woman spotted me through the glass and gave an imperious wave. I rushed to see what she wanted, eager to get on her good side.

"Have you asked if they have sparkling water?"

I fought a blush as I realized my mistake. Fortunately, the tour boat did stock it. I waved it like a trophy and set it before Cecilia.

"I need a glass, Megan."

"My name is Meg, Cecilia. I'm named after Meg Ryan."

That stirred her interest.

"My daughter was crazy about her. She was quite popular in the 90s." She squinted her eyes a bit. "Do I know you from somewhere?"

I had anticipated someone would ask this question a long time ago.

"You're from Colorado, aren't you? I've never been there."

She started telling me about their mountain town. I could tell she was warming up to me. Of course Mickey couldn't handle it.

"Get a glass," he ordered. "Never serve a drink without it, Meg. That's a no brainer."

He was annoying but also right. I jogged to the counter, asked for a clean glass and rushed back with it. On second thought, I went back and asked for a tray to go with the glass. I arrived with the empty glass on the tray and set it on the table with a flourish.

"Here you go, Cecilia. May I pour the water for you?"

"Mrs. Pierce," Mickey corrected me. "Our esteemed guest deserves your respect."

There was a buzz outside and the captain's voice filtered through the speakers. Eagles had been spotted, along with seals and he urged everyone to step out on deck for a bit. Mickey offered his arm to Cecilia Pierce but she grabbed mine.

"Megan can take me." She pinched my cheek. "You look just like that actress Cassie Butler. Before your time, of course. My daughter's a big fan."

She rambled about her middle aged daughter who was a successful realtor and very busy. I barely listened to her as we stepped outside and I watched bald eagles soaring in the skies around us, swaying on branches of tall firs. Ashley saw me and pointed at the shore where seals lined the rocks, basking in the watery sunlight.

The captain announced that a snacks table had been set up. I asked Cecilia if she wanted any.

"A little bit of everything." She perked up. "Get yourself a plate too. Young people need nourishment."

I wasn't going to argue with her. The buffet table had two bowls of salmon dip with an assortment of crackers. Loading two plates on a tray, I also filled two cups with hot chocolate and carried them to Cecilia. Mickey was on deck, schmoozing the green eyed man. Jeong Soo had his arm around the picky eater kid and they both held juice boxes. Ashley was nowhere to be seen.

Our next attraction was a collection of totem poles Ketchikan is famous for. Cecilia chose to stay inside this time, using binoculars to view the vibrant artifacts from Native American culture. How I wished I could take some pictures! Then I spotted Ashley.

"Where did you get that?" My mouth hung open when I saw the phone in her hand. "That's contraband."

"Let's take a selfie."

I didn't need a second invitation. We posed for several photos with the totem poles in the background. The captain announced our next stop, the first lighthouse ever built in Alaska.

The group was getting restless by the time the tour ended, talking about where to have lunch. I realized I hadn't had a timely meal since I boarded the ship. The captain recommended a few local restaurants just before the boat docked at the pier. Most of the people on the boat made a beeline for a local fish house that came highly recommended. Our group chose a more upscale restaurant a block down the road. I felt like I was entering a Dickensian world where we would be forced to stand and serve while the others ate their fill.

Mr. Green Eyes managed to shock the interns, even Mickey.

"Look, we're going to be stuck together for the rest of this cruise. So why don't you join us for lunch and tell us a bit about yourself?"

I ran a quick glance down the prices on the menu, putting on my poker face. Our host was either too rich or generous to a fault. The first I could imagine but the second I wasn't very sure about.

Chapter 6

We stood on Deck 2 at the ship's bow, talking about our day. It was my first experience of the midnight sun and it was a sight to behold.

The afternoon in Ketchikan had been grueling but fun. The group split up after we got back on board, the ladies heading to the spa. Cecilia Pierce wanted to rest so I took her to a secluded lounge and propped her up in a comfy chair, getting coffee and snacks. She told me I could take a short break.

I needed some iced coffee so I headed to the bar in the atrium on Deck 5. Mickey was already there, chatting up the bartender, the same one from the Sail Away party.

"Hey Nico!" I greeted him with a smile, letting him know there were no hard feelings.

Mickey looked at his watch and rapped his knuckles on the gleaming bar.

"Aren't you supposed to be at the bowling alley?"

RK had a special assignment for me. Mickey told me to rush to Deck 9 and go aft.

"That means at the back of the ship, right?" I asked him. "But what about Cecilia?"

Mickey promised to take care of her.

I spent the next thirty minutes scouring Deck 9, going aft first, then forward, then wondering if I had got the deck wrong. After examining every inch of Decks 7, 8 and 9, I finally took the help of a steward.

"Honey, there's no bowling alley on this ship."

I laughed all the way down to the dining room. Part of me wanted to throttle Mickey but I had to admit he wasn't boring. I would have to watch my step around him. The tour group was nowhere to be seen, neither were my fellow interns. I was debating having a quick snack when RK spotted me.

"You've got some nerve."

"I'm here to get pizza for the kid," I fibbed, crossing my fingers behind my back.

RK sighed deeply and shook her head. "The group is having dinner at the steakhouse and the other interns are seeing to their needs. Mrs. Pierce told me you just disappeared."

This was my opportunity to tell her about the nonexistent bowling alley but I'm not a snitch. So I let her words roll over me.

"Housekeeping needs help. You can work till midnight since you slacked off most of the day."

I headed to Housekeeping Central, trying to ignore the savory smells of chowder and fried fish wafting around me. Edna waited for me with a loaded cart. She dispatched me to Deck 7 with curt instructions to clean all the rooms. I don't think she recognized me.

Time had blurred as I vacuumed the worst kind of debris off the cabin floors, scrubbed toilets and wiped down surfaces. After what seemed like a lifetime, Edna appeared like an apparition, thanked me for my work and told me I could leave. Well, actually, she just said 'go' but I'm sure she meant all that.

I headed to the crew mess for some grub, thinking longingly of the hot tub in my Grandma's backyard. The interns sat at a table, eating berry pie. I loaded my plate with two slices of lasagna, a generous portion of Caesar salad and garlic bread. Then I spotted a roast chicken next to a pan of scalloped potatoes and decided to come back for it. I had definitely earned my supper.

"How old is that kid?" Ashley was asking Jeong Soo. "You seemed to get along well."

"Max knows my parents," he gushed, referring to the green eyed leader of the tour group. "He's met them at some medical conferences. I didn't realize he was that Maxwell Martin."

Jeong Soo went into raptures as he told us about the many tricky surgeries Dr. Maxwell Martin had performed, one even on the president of the United States. No wonder the whole group deferred to him.

"He must be loaded." Ashley seemed awed. "Did you see that dress his girl was wearing? Didn't come off a supermarket rack."

"So is our girl here." Mickey narrowed his eyes and pointed a finger at me. "You've been holding out on us, Meg."

He must have overheard Cecilia Pierce and put two and two together.

"I don't know what you mean." I chewed my salad, trying to look nonchalant.

"Really?" his eyes gleamed. "Tell us your mother's name."

"Cassandra Butler." I tasted the lasagna, waiting for some extreme reaction.

"Are we supposed to know her?" Ashley asked.

Mickey enlightened her.

"Cassie Butler is an award winning actress, Hollywood's darling. My mom's a big fan."

"Must be before my time," Ashley shrugged.

She was right. My mom had taken some time off so it was possible that kids my age didn't know her. But how could they not, I bristled with indignation, thinking about the superlative performances she had given in dozens of movies.

"You'll hear about her soon," I promised. "She's got the lead role in a new super hero movie that releases this Christmas."

Mickey was looking at me in a weird manner.

"The old lady was right. You do look like her. Wonder how I missed that."

He had been busy trying to wreck me, that's how.

"You must be rich too." Ashley's eyes were wide. "Why are you scrubbing toilets here, dude?"

Luca came in just then and she flew into his arms, saving me the need to reply.

Jeong Soo bid us good night. I thought Mickey would leave with him but he hadn't budged.

"Have you seen the midnight sun?" he leaned forward, joining his fingertips, looking uncertain. "There's a spot on Deck 2 where you can walk right up to the ship's bow. It's off limits to the cruisers."

I told him I would check it out sometime. Mickey's eyelids flickered and he leaned back, sliding lower in the booth.

"So I guess I'll see you tomorrow then? The train to White Horse Summit leaves at 7 AM sharp. Don't miss it."

"As long as we're not going on another boat!" I muttered. "See you tomorrow then, bright and early."

Ashley was busy cuddling with Luca so I made it to the cabin on my own. I had finally unpacked, glad

Grandma had talked me into carrying a little travel clock. It gave me a sense of time in the tin box that was my home for the next three months. I set the alarm and placed it on top of a cabinet, as far away from our bunks as possible so I wouldn't shut it off in my sleep.

The shrill alarm woke me up the minute I'd closed my eyes. I tried to make sense of the time through bleary eyes. Didn't clocks run faster in summer?

Ashley stirred on the bunk below and sat up with eyes closed, giving me dibs at the shower. She had somehow scored two mugs of steaming coffee by the time I came out, a towel wrapped around my body.

"Say thanks to Luca." She handed me a mug.

I liked cream in my coffee but it was better than nothing. Ashley was ready to go by the time I returned with some donuts from the crew mess. The ship was in dock and I was eager to explore Skagway.

We made it to the station with seconds to spare and boarded a toy like train. I pinched myself to see if I was dreaming.

"Have you ever been on a train?" I gushed, grabbing Ashley by the arms. "This is so exciting."

People walking through the town stopped to watch the train glide by and we waved at them. I wasn't sure where the train was going but I figured the cruise company had taken care of that.

"Let's track the others down." Ashley started walking down the car. "That lot is hard to miss."

We stalked to the end of the car, looking for our tour group. I realized we had entered the wrong car.

"This doesn't look good."

The train went around a steep bend just then. Ashley pointed at the snow tipped mountains in the distance and the Skagway river gurgling in the valley below.

"Don't worry about it." She sounded cool.

I decided to use the time to get to know her better.

"Where are you from?" I asked, stepping out on a viewing platform at the back of the car. "You never said anything."

"Nothing much to tell." Ashley grew serious. "My Mom died when I was four so I never knew her. Grandma raised me."

Her father had been a sailor, working for a cargo company. He had been away for most of the year.

"I was in my senior year in high school when the vessel he was on went missing." Ashley's eyes grew moist. "Grandma took it hard."

Ashley had finished one year of college when her grandmother was diagnosed with Alzheimer's. Her condition deteriorated rapidly until she had to be moved to a care facility.

"My college fund is barely enough to support us," Ashley sighed. "I work at the local diner at minimum wage."

Being a sailor's daughter, the high seas had always called to her.

"A job with a cruise line will ease a lot of our worries," she explained. "I'll get room and board and my salary will pay for Grandma's care."

I was no stranger to hardship so I offered my sympathy.

"What do you know?" she suddenly flared up. "Mickey said your mom's a Hollywood star. You guys must be rolling in millions."

"Not exactly."

I took a deep breath and plunged into my life story. Ashley's mouth dropped open when I told her how my mother had given me up for adoption.

"She was just 16," I explained. "And she had her own dreams. She believed I was better off with a loving family, one who actually needed a child."

"And were you?" Ashley stared at me in fascination.

My life hadn't turned out as expected. The first six years of my life must have been happy. I didn't remember much about them. Then my adoptive parents died in a car crash and I was put in the foster system. I had moved from one foster family to another 31 times until I got adopted again at sixteen.

"So a Hollywood star adopted you?" Ashley breathed. "Like Angelina Jolie, huh?"

I shook my head again. Cassie was my birth mom and I hadn't found her until I graduated high school.

"I took a gap year to track down my birth family. My grandma started looking for me around the same time."

Tiny streams rushed down the mountains as I narrated my life story. The train crossed a few bridges and went through a tunnel while Ashley sat rapt, engrossed in my story.

"You win!" she declared. "My life is so predictable compared to yours."

I had been processing Ashley's story in my mind as I told her about myself. If she was no longer in college, how had she managed to be chosen as an intern?

The train arrived at a station and we jumped off, anxious to catch up with the others. We looked inside every car but luck wasn't on our side.

"Where are they?" Ashley was frantic as we stood on the platform, our eyes searching the throng of people around us.

Mickey Singh had struck again. I couldn't believe I'd fallen for another one of his pranks.

Chapter 7

Ashley and I enjoyed our train ride to the Yukon Territory. The jaw dropping scenery made me fall in love with Alaska. Somehow, I had always imagined the frontier state to be gray and misty. The mountains swathed in greenery, the bright blue skies and the gushing rivers and streams in myriad shades of blue and green really surprised me. The ride had also given me a chance to bond with Ashley.

Our return in Skagway was kind of dull. We spotted our tour group as soon as we got off the train.

"Look who decided to show up," Mickey crowed, slapping Jeong Soo on the back.

Max Martin was not pleased with us. He let us know that by telling us to get our own lunch. The group stalked off to a fancy brewery, leaving us to our own devices. Mickey wasn't pleased.

"Look what you've done now!" he glared at me. "Lunch is gonna set me back twenty bucks."

I waved at the cruise ship docked beside us. He could go to the crew mess and grab a free meal. I didn't bring up the unnecessary train ride he'd sent us on, not willing to see him gloat.

Jeong Soo declared he was going with us.

"Let's eat that King Crab Alaska's famous for. My treat."

"Are you sure?" Ashley's eyes popped. "Maybe we can split it between us."

We chose a local café and ordered the crab, halibut cakes, salmon burgers and ended up sharing everything. Mickey hadn't joined us. He was probably off somewhere, planning another coup d'etat to get me kicked off the ship.

"How was your morning?" Ashley tasted a crab leg and pronounced it delicious.

Jeong Soo turned pale. He had accompanied Max Martin and his kid on a dog sledding excursion.

"A helicopter took us to the top of a glacier where we got on a sled pulled by dogs. It was horrible."

Ashley laughed goodnaturedly.

"Come on, live a little. You can't be squeamish if you want to be a doctor."

I wondered what Maxwell's wife and daughter had

been doing. Jeong Soo told us they had gone on a zip lining expedition. Most of the others had chosen to roam around the historic town.

We finished the food in record time and rushed out. None of us wanted to incur Maxwell's wrath. The afternoon was spent panning for gold. It was all make believe, of course, and a bit silly.

The group wanted to spend the last hour on shore at an open air café. Of course, the interns were expected to take orders, place them and then carry the drinks over to the entitled guests.

Cecilia Pierce asked for water. The café didn't carry the sparkling water she preferred. I scurried down the high street to a fancy pub, hoping to strike pay dirt. A brown haired man sat with her when I returned, sweating profusely. He was the man in the pink shirt I had noticed yesterday.

"Can I get you a lemonade?" I asked him. "Something to cool you down?"

He seemed to cower before me.

"Edmund's a bit shy," Cecilia told me. "Best leave him alone."

Soon, it was time to get back to the ship. Maxwell's wife wanted another massage.

"Can you go to Guest Services and book an appointment for me?" she asked. "Not now, maybe in two hours? I need a nap first."

I watched her tall, voluptuous figure as she walked toward a bank of elevators, barely acknowledging my nod. She seemed a lot younger than Max Martin.

"Trophy wife, I bet," Ashley spoke in my ear. "She's not old enough to have a teenaged daughter."

I spied RK talking to Max Martin. Would he squeal on us?

Some of the group chose to have an early dinner at the grand buffet, giving us a chance to work on our waitressing skills. Others had reservations at the piano bar or were ordering room service.

"You should've listened to me, Dani." The jock I had noticed hanging around Max's daughter wailed. "What could be more romantic than dinner on the balcony, enjoying this great view?"

"Dad will ground me forever if I come to your cabin alone."

"He doesn't have to know," the boy wheedled. "Why are you so afraid of him?"

"Because …" The Martin girl wouldn't say any more.

My mind was buzzing with many scenarios. Max sounded like an old fossil. Was he just a tough parent or something more? I didn't like the fear I saw in his daughter's eyes.

The sweaty man from the afternoon mopped his brow and told the jock to stop bothering the girl. I didn't miss the grateful look Dani flashed him. Max held up his hand just then and I rushed toward him, eager to butter him up.

"What can I get you, Sir?"

"You can call me Max. Say, what's that rascal saying to my daughter? Up to no good, I bet."

Did he seriously expect me to spy on the poor girl? I told him I hadn't been paying attention.

He slipped me a twenty and told me I could get more if I kept an eye on Dani.

"I worry about her, you know. She puts on a big act but she's just a child."

Call me sentimental, but I could've hugged him then. I had no firsthand experience of how protective a father could be. Dani didn't know how lucky she was.

The Martin kid wanted a banana split and Jeong Soo volunteered to get it for him. The others wanted to try a variety of the desserts offered so Ashley and I loaded two trays with slices of caramel cheesecake, wild berry cobbler, chocolate chunk cookies and a lemon coconut cake. Max was the only one who wanted an after dinner espresso.

It was almost 9 PM when the group dismissed us for the day. I heard Dani and the jock whispering about meeting up outside the theater in thirty minutes. I guessed they had planned to sneak out to watch some adult entertainment. The crisp twenty dollar bill in my pants pocket needled my conscience and I struggled to decide what the right thing was. Should I tell Max about his daughter's nocturnal plans?

Mickey reminded us we still had to meet RK. He looked excited, probably because he expected to be at the top of the leader board yet again. I had no doubt he was right and braced myself for a fresh reprimand.

RK sat in her cabin, her feet resting on a low stool. Her ears turned red when I entered with Ashley.

"You!" she jabbed a finger in my direction. "You're going to cost me this job. Do you know how hard I've worked to be Training Manager?"

My eyes met Ashley's and a silent message passed between us. I was going to let her field this one.

"We are sorry for the mix up," she sputtered. "We presumed the whole group was going on the White Pass train ride."

RK's foot landed on the floor with a thud.

"What's this? Some new mess you girls got into?"

So the RK monster had not heard about our train excursion.

Jeong Soo was staring at the leader board, his eyes wide with fear. I noticed Mickey had turned red. I followed their gaze and couldn't hold back a smile. Kim Jeong Soo topped the chart, followed by Ashley and Mickey. I wasn't surprised to see myself at the bottom.

"This board is all wrong," Mickey blurted. "How did

the Korean kid go to the top?"

RK told us Max Martin couldn't stop singing Jeong Soo's praises. He had really bonded with the Martin boy, leaving his parents free to enjoy the cruise.

"That's because the Kim and Martin families know each other," Mickey snarled. "This is nepotism."

"Is that true?" RK asked Jeong Soo. "Have you ever met these people before now?"

Tongue tied, Jeong Soo shook his head. Ashley came to his rescue.

"Max Martin is a famous doctor. So are Jeong Soo's parents."

RK barely heard her, training her eyes on me again. I was back in the hot seat.

"Do you realize your pranks can cause serious harm? I'm not talking about the money the cruise line stands to lose when a guest badmouths us. No, no. What about the bodily harm you can cause to the guests?"

I tried to work out what she meant but I was clueless.

"What have I done now?" I got straight to the point. "You don't have to sugar coat it for me."

There was a limit to my patience too, after all. I was sleep and food deprived and had been the victim of several silly pranks. I decided it was time to step up and be more assertive. Clearly, it wasn't the right approach with her.

RK crossed her arms across her ample chest and struggled to speak. Her blood pressure must have been off the charts.

"You put soiled sheets in the guest rooms last night."

"What?" I shrieked, unable to handle this latest allegation. "What makes you say that?"

Mickey sniggered, earning a dark look from RK.

"I just took the housekeeping cart from Edna," I told her. "All the sheets I changed were freshly laundered. I'm sure whoever complained is just trying to fleece the cruise company."

RK wasn't buying it. I tried to think back to the previous evening. Could one of the dozens of sheets I changed have had a stain?

"It's not just a tiny stain either." RK managed to shock me again. "One of them had body fluids and three of them had been smeared with peanut butter. Fortunately for you, none of the people in those rooms were allergic."

"I'm being set up." I swallowed. "Surely you realize this?"

"Why should I believe you, Margaret?" RK shot back. "First the tampered drinks, now this! Do you realize if the captain hears about this, he'll throw you in the brig?"

I wondered if the prison facilities on the ship were more spacious than my stamp sized cabin. This internship was turning out to be a disaster.

"Third strike and you're out," RK warned me. "I can't encourage this kind of destructive behavior but I dare not put you on housekeeping duty again."

I was dispatched to clean the staff and crew quarters. One look at Mickey's grin told me it was going to be a nightmare. Ashley took my arm when we filed out of RK's office.

"Let's grab a bite first. She can't let you starve. You have some rights too, you know."

I didn't think RK Powell was concerned about my rights. If she was, she wouldn't have been so quick to pin the blame on me. She couldn't actually have any proof since I was innocent. Although she was unfair, I understood her predicament.

Why was I being targeted? Sending us on a wild goose chase was one thing. Deliberately putting the passengers in danger pointed to a really desperate individual. And I knew only person who had made no secret of his dislike for me.

Was winning the internship prize so important to Mickey?

Chapter 8

The next day was a sailing day where the ship would visit some glaciers. For many, this was the highlight of the trip. Ashley was looking forward to it but I was too exhausted to care.

"You poor thing," she clucked as we sat in the crew mess, drinking coffee. "Let me get you something to eat."

I was nauseous after the filth I had waded through the previous night. A glass of juice was all I could stomach.

"Most of the toilets weren't even flushed," I sobbed. "What kind of people are we working with, Ash?"

"Maybe it's a culture thing," she shrugged. "So, you think we'll get a chance to go up on the deck?"

The answer to that was no. The tour group had already decided to split up. Max and his family had chosen to go out in the open, along with another couple. The jock went with them so I presumed they must be his parents. Cecilia Pierce preferred to be at the closed, temperature controlled observation deck.

"The cold's bad for my hip," she told me. "Jackie and Edmund will keep me company."

Edmund was dressed for the outdoors, bundled up in a thick sweater and had wrapped a cashmere scarf round his neck. He didn't look pleased. My guess was Cecilia had nixed his plans.

"A little fresh air is good for you," he ventured. "Just think of all the sights we came here to see, soaring mountains, wildlife, glaciers. Just give it a chance."

Cecilia wasn't buying it.

"You can go if you want. No need to babysit an old lady."

"It's no trouble," the woman with them cooed.

She was a brunette with blonde highlights in her hair and a heavy figure. She could stand to lose twenty pounds but was no less attractive.

"I'm Jackie," she introduced herself. "Jackie Solano. You're doing a great job taking care of us."

Obviously, she was a sycophant. I preferred Maxwell's direct approach to her silver tongue. He might have tried to bribe me but at least he was a straight shooter. It didn't take me two minutes to realize Jackie was a clinger. She had some vested interest in sucking up to Cecilia Pierce.

I made sure the café at the observation deck had a supply of sparkling water. Jackie wanted a cappuccino. Edmund sat with his back to the ladies, staring outside, sulking like a kid who had been punished and asked to go to his room. Why didn't he just get up and go where he wanted?

The ship was traveling through Glacier Bay that day. I sat with my back to the windows, giving Cecilia a foot massage. She exclaimed every time we came across some waterfall, or spotted harbor seals or a bear traipsing across the mountains. After an hour or so, she finally gave me a break so I could stand close to the windows, taking my first glimpse of the untouched beauty surrounding us.

Soon it was noon and time for lunch. The group had booked a table in the big dining room. There was plenty of wait staff so Max gave us a reprieve.

Ashley proposed going to the buffet. Mickey and Jeong Soo agreed readily. They had spent the morning outside and were hankering for a hot meal.

One of the guys at the buffet station recommended the seafood chowder so I decided to try it, along with grilled salmon salad and crab cakes. Mickey was quiet. Either he repented giving me a hard time or he was engrossed in putting away the mountain of food before him. Ashley took pity on me.

"Let's swap places, Meg. Tori Martin will run you ragged but at least you'll be able to get some fresh air. It's freezing out there, though."

I saw RK enter the buffet area and warned the others. She gave us a wave and went to the salad station. Jeong Soo gobbled his chicken nuggets and stood up, ready to bolt.

"Don't leave on my account, kid." RK pulled up a chair and sat down.

So she wasn't going to eat us alive.

"The internship program is my baby." She speared a piece of blackened chicken and dipped it in a sticky bourbon sauce. "It's just a small part of my other duties."

Ashley stole a glance at me, an unspoken question in her eyes. Like me, she was trying to guess what was coming.

"My interns and I have a lot of fun each summer," RK continued. "You might find that hard to believe, Margaret."

"Meg," I prompted. "My name is Meg."

I don't think she heard me.

"We got off on the wrong foot. But what was I supposed to do? First you arrive ten hours late, then you almost poison the passengers." She gave a tiny shrug. "What I'm saying is, let's start over."

Getting my name right seemed like a good starting point.

"You don't mean that." I almost asked her what her game was.

RK told us she was sincere. She wanted us to enjoy the summer. Of course, we would be working our butts off, working in different areas across the ship. But she wanted us to have a good time while doing it.

All of us nodded, dumbstruck. Even Mickey didn't say a thing.

RK proposed dinner at one of the specialty restaurants that night, a sort of 'welcome to the Silver

Queen' party.

"But what about the tour group?" Jeong Soo mumbled.

RK told us she would take care of it.

The day was suddenly looking up. RK didn't stay for dessert but insisted we try a special bread pudding topped with local Alaska strawberries. We agreed to meet her at the restaurant five minutes before 8 PM.

I couldn't believe my luck when Cecilia declared she was going to her cabin for a nap. Max had taken his family to a trivia contest. Ashley and I hopped with excitement as we rushed to the bow of the ship to see the sights.

The next hour was a revelation. The water around us was littered with chunks of ice of different sizes. Ashley told me they were called bergy bits. Someone pointed out a mountain goat on land. The day was bright but chilly and almost everyone had accepted the blankets the staff was handing out. I spotted Edmund in a corner, sipping a cup of hot chocolate. Jackie stood beside him, talking his head off. Even from a distance, I could tell he had tuned her out.

"They are like two ends of a pole," Ashley

murmured.

"And opposites attract," I reminded her.

"You mean they are sweet on each other?"

I paused to think for a minute, then shook my head.

"He's just being polite. I think Edmund is a bit of an introvert."

Ashley thought he was kind of rude. He had walked to the port side while we were talking, leaving Jackie on her own. She saw us watching her so we had to go and say hello.

"Can I get you anything?" I asked her. "One more blanket? More coffee?"

She shook her head.

"How long have you worked for the cruise line?" she wanted to know.

I pointed to our uniforms which were different from the rest of the staff.

"We are interns," I told her. "Just here for the summer."

"I could never afford a cruise like this." Ashley confessed she came from a meager background.

Jackie placed a hand on her arm.

"You have nothing to apologize for. But don't let your beginnings define where you want to go in life."

The fervor in her voice was unexpected. I was willing to bet Jackie came from a poor family herself.

We chatted with her for some time. After a while, the cold became unbearable and we decided to go inside. Ashley was meeting Luca at a café on a lower deck. She dragged me along.

"Is this serious?" I asked. "What do you know about Luca?"

"Don't worry, Mom!" she rolled her eyes. "I'm just having some fun."

I held my hands up and backed off. Ashley and I were practically strangers and she wouldn't appreciate my meddling in her personal life.

Luca was waiting for us. He gallantly offered to fetch our coffee.

"Let me do it," I said. "You look exhausted."

He gave in easily and thanked me. The poor guy had been chopping vegetables since six in the morning. I was glad I hadn't been put on kitchen duty.

I didn't want to be a third wheel so I got the drinks and made an excuse to leave. Luca urged me to hang out with them.

"When did you come to the United States?" I asked him.

He had been hired in Europe and then traveled wherever the ship went until his contract ran out. He had worked for many different cruise lines and sailed from American ports.

"I never actually lived in the US," he explained. "When I get some time off, I go home to Roma."

"I'm Italian too, you know," I smiled.

His face seemed to crumple for a split second.

"How is that?"

"Part Italian, I guess," I shrugged. "My grandma's parents were Italian."

"No wonder you're so passionate about this job," he marked.

Ashley gave a yelp and pointed at a clock on the wall. It was ten past seven. We needed to head to the cabin and get ready for dinner.

I pulled out a short black frock that belonged to my mother. It was her lucky dress and she had entrusted it in my care for the summer. She had also lent me a silk scarf in shades of aquamarine. I thought it was perfect for the occasion.

Ashley did her makeup in the tiny bathroom while I changed. Then we swapped places. I felt a rumble in my stomach. Before I knew it, bile rose up my throat and I barely made it to the toilet bowl.

"You okay?" Ashley knocked on the door.

I was kind of embarrassed and I didn't want to worry her so I told her I was fine. Ashley wore a red jumpsuit that set off her jet black hair and vivid blue eyes. Together, we made a striking pair.

We made it to the restaurant with five minutes to spare. Jeong Soo had arrived before us, dressed in a natty dark suit.

"You must be a heart breaker back home." Ashley smoothed his hair.

Mickey arrived, wearing a sports coat. He didn't look pleased to see me. RK arrived before he could make a snarky comment.

"Good evening, young ones!" she beamed. "You make me proud." She gave me a onceover. "Chanel and Hermes? You sure have taste, Margaret."

I opened my mouth to correct her.

"Meg," she said and smiled.

I thanked her and told her it was just something old from my mother's closet.

"Vintage Chanel is still Chanel," she grinned. "Your mother has exquisite taste."

Mickey was biting his lip, probably jealous of the attention RK was giving me. I decided to ignore him.

A table had been reserved for us and the meal already ordered. There was a bunch of balloons by our table and a cake with 'Welcome' written on it in frosting. RK had really made an effort.

The meal started with cioppino, a kind of Italian seafood soup. It was one of my favorites. A low rumble started in my stomach and I looked around in desperation, trying to spot an exit sign or a restroom.

"Are you alright?" Ashley clutched my hand, her voice full of concern. "I heard you puking your guts out earlier."

RK's eyes widened. She threw her napkin on the table and came around to my side.

"Let's go," she hissed in my ear, grabbing my arm in a manner I was getting used to.

I was in no position to argue. We reached a restroom in the nick of time. RK was pacing the floor and muttering to herself when I did my business and came out.

"Why didn't you tell me you were sick?"

In truth, I have an iron constitution so the thought that something might be wrong had never entered my mind.

"It's okay," I assured her, touched by her concern. "I brought some Pepto with me. I'll be fine by morning."

"You silly girl!" she slapped her palm on her forehead. "This is what happens when you don't attend orientation."

Apparently, all employees were supposed to report an upset stomach immediately and go to the infirmary. I had committed a major faux pas once again, managing to lose any goodwill I might have earned with RK.

Chapter 9

Dinner was forgotten as I was dispatched to the infirmary or sick bay on Deck 2. A gruff East European with mutton chop whiskers asked me delicate questions about how many times I had purged the contents of my stomach that day. He was very curious to know when it all started. Ashley was subjected to the same interrogation.

RK sent us to our rooms after that and told us to stay put until further notice. Our meals would be delivered to our rooms. The life of an intern couldn't get more luxurious on the Silver Queen. I was too exhausted to wonder what was happening and fell asleep as soon as my head hit the thin pillow.

The morning brought some clarity. I sat up in my bunk, rubbing my eyes, looking around for my alarm clock. Instead, my gaze landed on Ashley, lounging on a tiny stool in her pajamas.

"It's ten past nine," she told me. "We're allowed to sleep in today 'coz we're not leaving this tiny prison cell."

I spied two breakfast trays on the table next to Ashley and jumped down. There was juice, coffee and a bowl of thin oatmeal.

"What's this?" I grumbled. "I'm starving. Can't we ask for some eggs and toast? Or pancakes?"

The meal was tailored for my upset stomach.

"Soft food only. Doctor's orders." Ashley explained we had been put in a sort of quarantine. "Norovirus! That's what they are afraid of."

Apparently, it was a virus that could spread very fast and infect a lot of people. They would raise the alarm if anyone else reported sick and strict protocols would kick in. RK had grilled me for a long time, asking if I had remembered to wash and sanitize my hands.

"What about the Hubbard Glacier?" I was dismayed.

"As far as I know, it's still standing."

"Ha, ha!" I made a face at Ashley. "Does this mean we can't go out and see it?"

She was more worried about missing a date with Luca.

"He had promised to take me to lunch. Not

happening, I guess!"

"Do you know the Hubbard Glacier has been around for five hundred years?" I cried. "Maybe even more. I've always wanted to see it."

Ashley told me to relax. The ship would be taking the same route multiple times that summer. I was bound to get another opportunity to watch that hunk of ice.

I drained the glass of orange juice and chose to sulk. Ashley put on headphones and ignored me. Time crawled at a snail's place. We got chicken soup for lunch with half a baguette each. Jeong Soo knocked on our door sometime in the afternoon. He wanted to know how I was feeling.

"Are you supposed to be here?" I asked, touched by his concern. "What if RK sees you?"

"Mickey and I decided to risk it," he whispered.

I couldn't believe Mickey was outside my door. Maybe he had a heart. The boys wanted to know if we wanted anything.

"Coffee and cake sounds good," I told them. "And maybe something solid for dinner, like chicken tenders or a cheeseburger."

Jeong Soo promised he would talk to someone in the kitchen. He was true to his word. We got chicken tenders for dinner, with a chipotle dipping sauce and garlic mashed potatoes. There was a tiny piece of apple pie for each of us. The whole meal had the appeal of forbidden fruit and tasted delicious.

RK arrived some time after nine.

"I have good news. Nobody else has been sick so your symptoms are isolated."

She wanted to know how I was feeling.

"I'm fine," I assured her. "Just tired of being cooped up in here."

"Why don't you see the doctor again?" she coaxed. "Let him examine you once more."

I told her I didn't mind going to sick bay but there was nothing wrong with me. The doctor hadn't given me any medicine anyway. I had gulped down some Pepto before going to bed and I was fine. No puking incidents, no stomach pain or nausea.

"That's excellent!" RK looked relieved. "I guess you can go out on deck now, get some fresh air. But no partying."

I could tell Ashley didn't like the sound of that. RK reminded us we had to catch the train to Denali in the morning. She advised us to get a good night's sleep because we would be on our feet for the entire nine hour journey.

Ashley put on a fresh coat of lipstick the moment RK left us. I didn't have to guess where she was headed. A bit of solitude sounded good to me.

Although the sun was still visible, the temperatures had dropped a lot. I shivered in my parka and decided to walk around to keep warm. Other like minded passengers were doing the same. Couples cuddled by the railing, admiring the three sixty degree views around us. Ribbons of peach and pink adorned the sky and the water shimmered in the slanting rays. My face was frozen very soon and I decided to head back after finishing one loop.

A familiar figure sat in a deck chair, swathed in a thick winter coat and Eskimo hat. I stopped to say Hello. It was one of the things I had picked up from the Orientation manual that afternoon.

"Lovely evening."

Edmund nodded without saying a word.

"Can I get you anything?" I asked. "Some coffee or hot chocolate?"

There was a small kiosk at one end of the deck where a crew member was dispensing hot drinks. Edmund gave a slight nod but didn't specify what he wanted. I made an executive decision and got him a mug of hot chocolate with marshmallows. It was a wrong move.

He thanked me and began fishing out the marshmallows.

"Don't like 'em," he mumbled.

I rushed back to get him another drink minus the marshmallows.

"My mom likes to put six marshmallows in hers," I told him.

"You look like her." He managed to surprise me. "Spitting image of her in her 20s."

Edmund admitted he was a Cassie Butler fan. He had watched every film of hers dozens of times and was eagerly waiting for her new superhero movie.

"You have her passion, kid. I think you'll go places."

I returned to the cabin with a big smile on my face. Ashley was out and I didn't expect her back until the early hours of the morning. I packed a small duffel bag with enough clothes for three days and hit the sack.

For once, I woke before my tiny alarm clock chimed. I was that excited to go to Denali. Ashley was in her bunk, fully dressed. She had probably planned it so she could sleep in until the last moment. I hummed in the shower and headed to the mess for breakfast. Jeong Soo was eating a ham omelet that looked appealing so I got the same, along with a bagel and smoked salmon and a bowl of fruit.

"Where's Mickey?" I asked him.

"He was already gone when I woke up." Jeong Soo shrugged. "Don't know where he is half the time."

"Good for us," I laughed. "You looking forward to our trip?"

He was hoping to catch Max Martin in a good mood so he could pick his brain.

"I can ask him about medical school."

"Isn't that four years away?"

"Three if I'm on fast track. Max can advise me on which courses to take in college. I'm already taking piano lessons."

I sensed he was going to launch into an explanation on how the piano would help him become a better surgeon. Mickey's arrival saved me.

"You're at the bottom of the leader board again, Meg."

Judging by the way things were going, I would never get off it. I wasn't going to let it bother me.

Mickey said he had already eaten although he didn't explain when and where. We trooped to RK's office, Ashley joining us at the last minute.

"I have never let interns take overnight excursions." RK cleared her throat. "This is a new itinerary for the cruise line and I need you to be on your best behavior."

She was going to come along to make sure we didn't mess up. I was relieved. None of the four interns was experienced enough to handle a real emergency.

We made a quick trip to our cabins to get our bags and took the elevator to the deck where the disembarkation had already begun. RK strode ahead and we trotted after her, eager to please.

The tour group stood at an assigned spot with their luggage. Cecilia leaned on her cane with a pained expression on her face.

"What's taking him so long, Max?" she grumbled.

RK took a quick roll call and realized Edmund hadn't joined them yet.

"Where is Mr. Toole?" she asked the group. "According to my records, he is part of the Denali excursion."

Jackie wondered if he had overslept. I was dispatched to go check on him. RK asked Mickey to go with me.

"What if he's not ready?" I asked him as we rode the elevator to Edmund's cabin. "Aren't we running late?"

Mickey thought the cruise line might hold the train back for a few minutes but I wasn't too sure.

We located Edmund Toole's cabin and I knocked on his door, softly at first and then a bit louder. Mickey told me to step aside after five minutes and started banging on the door with his fist.

"I think we should call security."

He took my hand in his and we ran down the corridor, trying to spot a crew member who might have a walkie talkie on them. Security arrived ten minutes later and used their pass key, telling us to wait four doors down. Things happened very fast after that. Four more security guys materialized. One of them told us to move further back while another spoke in his walkie.

"Alpha, alpha, alpha."

The orientation manual was fresh in my mind and I gasped as I remembered what it meant.

"Is Edmund ill?" I asked the guard. "But he was fine last night."

The gruff European doctor with the mutton chops arrived at a run and went into the cabin. One of the guards escorted us from the floor. I heard one of his colleagues speak in his walkie again, mentioning a bright star.

My heart skipped a beat as I made the connection again. I squeezed Mickey's hand and stared at him, unable to believe what was happening. His shoulders slumped and he gave a slight nod, confirming my suspicion.

"Edmund is dead."

Chapter 10

Mickey and I sat at a table in the main dining room, surrounded by concerned people. For once, we were the ones being catered to. Ashley stood behind me, her hands on my shoulders, offering silent support. Jeong Soo looked like he might burst into tears any moment. The tour group sat a few feet away from us.

RK made us drink coffee with plenty of cream and sugar. Max Martin had rushed down to Edmund's room when he learned what happened.

"I was afraid of this," I heard him mutter.

What did he mean? Was Edmund Toole suffering from some grave disease? Had he been on his last legs?

The coffee was too sweet for me but I took a few sips under RK's watchful eye. Fortunately, I had been spared the sight of a dead body. I was in shock, I think, too stunned to know how or what I felt.

"Can we have some breakfast?" Tori Martin asked RK. "We had planned to eat on the train."

Max arrived before RK could reply.

"Edmund's gone alright." His tone was gruff. "Died in his sleep so he didn't suffer."

RK looked at her watch and stood up.

"We need to get going, unless you want to cancel your trip to Denali and stay on the ship for three days."

I couldn't believe what I was hearing. Could they be so callous?

"I don't know about the rest," Max gave a shrug. "But I don't see any reason to change my plans. Do you know how many patients I had to shuffle to clear this time on my schedule?"

"We didn't really know him," another woman spoke up. "He was practically a stranger to us."

The rest of the tour group murmured amongst themselves. Jackie spoke for them.

"Max is right. This is a once in a lifetime trip for most of us. Let's get going."

There was a flurry of activity as RK ordered us to help carry luggage. I hefted a large duffel bag on my shoulder and dragged two large suitcases, allowing

Cecilia to lean on my arm. A special ramp was cleared so we could disembark without any more delay. The group had booked a private coach to take them to the train station.

Ashley and I had barely exchanged a word since morning. We finally got a chance to talk after the group boarded the train.

"You're not happy," she mused. "But you also don't seem surprised. Are all rich people so cold hearted?"

I told her about the cruise I had been on before.

"The cruise line doesn't like to advertise these things. And Max gave them what they need on a platter. If he says Edmund had a heart attack, why would the ship's doctor challenge him?"

Ashley frowned. "That's not what I meant. Are you saying there is something suspicious about the man's death?"

"I ran into him on deck last night, less than eight hours ago. He was perfectly fine then, Ash."

She told me she was talking about the group's lack of emotion.

"Not a single one of them seems sad."

She thought someone would shed a tear for poor Edmund. But we barely knew the group. Based on what I had observed in the last few days, Edmund Toole had been a loner. He may not have been close to his neighbors.

"He did come on this tour," Ashley reminded me. "Why would he do that if he didn't know them well?"

RK interrupted our tete a tete.

"Start serving breakfast, girls."

Any notion I might have had of standing on the viewing platform, admiring the scenery around us, was dashed.

"The train is fully staffed, RK. They should be serving us."

RK laughed until tears rolled down her eyes.

"Did you think you were going to put your feet up and gaze at the mountains, Margaret?"

Well, when she put it that way …

112

"Just look around us." I waved a hand at the view outside the window. "Can you blame me for thinking I was on vacation?"

We encountered Mickey and Jeong Soo on our way to the upper deck of the car. They were two steps ahead and had already asked the group for their breakfast orders. We trooped to the dining car.

"Let's divide and conquer," I suggested. "Jeong Soo, you handle all the juices. Ashley can do the tea and coffee. Mickey and I will carry the food."

We had to do multiple trips. Dani and her mother Tori ordered stuffed French Toast. My mouth watered as I smelt the vanilla wafting off the chunky bread, smothered in strawberry compote, dusted with sugar.

"You think we'll get breakfast?" I asked Mickey. "I could use a bite."

He thought RK would allow us to grab a packed sandwich or something. I set a breakfast platter before Cecilia Pierce. She and Jackie had ordered the country breakfast with scrambled eggs, reindeer sausage, home fries and wheat toast.

"Why do I get only one sausage?" the old woman

pointed at Jackie's plate. "She's got two."

I was dumbstruck. Was she insinuating I stole her food?

Mickey stood behind her, trying to hold back a smirk. It didn't take me long to figure out what had happened.

"We're not allowed to eat off the passengers' plates, Meg." Mickey acted shocked. "Surely you know that?"

RK came by to check on the passengers. I'm sure Mickey had seen her coming before he made that atrocious statement.

"Everything alright here?" RK was giving me a hard look.

Cecilia pushed her plate away and tapped her cane.

"Your girl mooched something off my plate. Don't you feed your employees?"

Jackie cajoled her to calm down. I offered to get her an extra helping of the sausages. RK asked me to apologize.

"I didn't steal your food," I began indignantly and saw RK shaking her head, glaring at me. "But I do apologize for the inconvenience."

That would have to do.

RK told me to take a break. I rushed to the viewing platform and stood there, clutching the bars, feeling the cold wind caress my face. Ashley joined me there.

"We have fifteen minutes," she told me. "RK wants us to fetch tea or coffee after that."

I gave Mickey a wide berth when we went inside. There was no doubt he took every opportunity to discredit me. So I was surprised when he owned up to me.

"I popped a sausage in my mouth," he confessed. "I was starving."

Hunger was something I had a lot of experience with. It was nothing to joke about.

"That's okay," I shrugged. "But why didn't you say that in front of RK?"

Mickey told me he wasn't that crazy.

We took orders for drinks and made sure our group didn't want anything else. Someone must have brought up Edmund. Jackie was roasting him when I set her coffee before her.

"He was so rude," she clucked. "Absolutely no manners, you know. I wonder why he came on this trip with us."

A homely, middle aged woman with some gray at her temples defended Edmund.

"Come on, Jackie. Cut him some slack, would you? The poor man's dead."

"I call it like it is." Jackie took a sip of her coffee and wrinkled her nose. "There's no sugar in my coffee." She saw me and snapped her fingers. "Can you get me two sugars?"

I pointed to the packets of sugar I had placed on a small plate next to the coffee. Jackie wasn't pleased. She tore two packets open at once and stirred her drink with a bit too much force.

"Where was I?" She stared at the woman she was talking to. "Edmund Toole was uncouth. I don't care if I'm the only one who's willing to say it out loud."

"Don't you find his death fishy though?" I asked. "He was young and healthy, he hardly looked like he'd keel over."

Jackie gave me a look. She was probably the kind of snob who did not like to fraternize with the help. I wasn't shocked when she thrust her coffee cup in my hands and stalked away.

"Edmund was shy," the older woman with Jackie said with a sigh. "He was an introvert, plain and simple."

"That explains it," I nodded.

The woman introduced herself as Ruth Heinzman. She was the jock's mother.

"People are often mistaken about shy people," she sighed. "It's their egos, you know. Don't like being ignored."

I tried to read between the lines. Was she trying to tell me something?

"Are you saying Edmund ignored Jackie on purpose?"

"I wouldn't say that." She clammed up. "The truth is,

Edmund Toole was a loner. My husband and I were surprised to see him on this trip."

"You must've seen him around the neighborhood, cycling or going for a run."

I was rewarded with the information I wanted.

"He wasn't the active type, I think. We had a 5K run in our county last year to support the local food bank. A bunch of people from our neighborhood made up a team. Every person contributed a hundred bucks to be on it. I remember Edmund paid the money but opted out of the event."

So Edmund could have had health issues.

"Did he have a bad heart?" I asked. "He wasn't obese so the 5K shouldn't have been too difficult for him."

She thought the group activity had been the real deterrent but she couldn't say for sure. Jackie came back to her seat and asked for water. I brought her a cold bottle and escaped, hoping to grab a bite.

Ashley and the interns sat at a table in the dining car, a wide variety of dishes before them. RK wanted us to sample everything so we would be able to recommend dishes and answer any questions the passengers may have about the food.

Jeong Soo ate a porridge made of barley, topped with fresh berries and honey. Ashley had a plate of French toast before her. Mickey was demolishing the big breakfast platter. I picked up a fork and tucked in. We decided to rate the food and the French toast came out at top. The reindeer sausage didn't go down well with Jeong Soo and Ashley. I thought it was worth a shot since it was the local specialty.

"How long is this train ride?" I wanted to know, appalled to hear it would take us eight hours to reach Denali. "Are we supposed to be on our feet all the time?"

"Get used to it," Ashley quipped. "Crews often work fourteen or sixteen hours with no time off for months."

I wondered if I might have to rethink the whole working on a cruise ship thing. Picking grapes in Tuscany sounded easy compared to this.

"What's the matter?" Mickey put his hands behind his head. "You ready to catch a flight back home?"

I wasn't going to fold that easily and I told him that.

"You served Max and his family, didn't you?" I asked. "Did he say anything about Edmund?"

Ashley wanted to know why I was obsessed with the dead guy. She was trying her best to forget the whole episode.

"He was a human being, Ash." I tried to stay calm. "Everyone just wants to sweep him under a rug."

Mickey gave a shrug and turned away, admiring the waterfalls cascading down the mountains. It was his way of saying he couldn't care less.

"I have a gut feeling about this," I persisted. "My instincts have never steered me wrong."

Indeed, they had saved me in many a sticky situation.

"Spill it, Megs!" Ashley's brow furrowed. "What's on your mind?"

"Did Edmund Toole really die a natural death?" I paused for dramatic effect. "I don't think so."

Chapter 11

The brief respite we had coincided with a stop at Talkeetna, a quaint town known as the gateway to Denali. Ashley and I stood on the tiny viewing platform between two cars, unaware of the fantastic scenery in store for us. The train turned around a steep bend and Mount Denali loomed in the distance. I forgot everything, feasting my eyes on the tall, snowcapped peaks that filled my vision, glad I didn't have any phone or camera to distract me.

RK arrived and clapped her hands, telling us it was time to serve lunch. The tour group was seated in the dining car, perusing menus. Many of them opted for the pasta with reindeer Bolognese sauce. Fish and chips made with fresh, local cod was the other popular dish. Cecilia was the only one who chose pot roast.

We had each been assigned a couple of tables. I was in charge of the Martin family. I served drinks and carried their food over. The young kid grabbed his milkshake and almost upset it, earning a reprimand from his father. Maxwell cut his fish with gusto, thanking me for my service.

"How did Edmund die?" I decided to capitalize on

his good mood.

He seemed surprised by the question.

"Edmund Toole was under medication." He cleared his throat. "It's most likely that he had a fatal heart attack."

How could he be so sure?

"So, a cardiac event was a known side effect of the medicine he was taking?"

Max poured ketchup over his fries and stopped to check on his son's food. I watched as he cut the boy's chicken into pieces, exhibiting a tender side.

"Why are you asking this?"

As usual, I didn't think much before speaking.

"I mean, did he switch medicines recently? Was this a known side effect of the meds he was on?"

Max took a couple more bites of his fish, making me wonder if he had heard.

"Come on, Max! Are you sure Edmund's death was natural? You don't suspect any foul play?"

He set his soda down and wiped his mouth, unable to hide his mirth.

"You kids! What is this? Some kind of conspiracy theory to liven things up?"

I told him I was very serious. Edmund's death was too sudden.

Max turned toward his son again, forcing him to eat the two florets of broccoli that had come with the chicken.

"Improbable," he nodded. "But not impossible. Nothing in life is certain, Meg."

His nostrils flared and his eyes flickered. I realized I had stirred a painful memory.

"My advice to you, as a doctor and parent and someone old enough to be your Pop, live it up while you can, kid. Life can turn upside down in a minute."

RK materialized at my shoulder. She had a knack of doing that.

"Everything alright here, Dr. Martin?" She assessed the situation swiftly. "Can Margaret here get you something? More coffee, perhaps?"

No mere mortal could say no to the RK monster. The entire Martin family wanted drink refills and guess who was responsible for getting them?

"We don't fraternize with the guests." RK took me to task later, after I delivered the drinks and got a second bowl of ice cream for the Martin kid. "There is a zero tolerance policy on this one."

"I thought fraternize means something else." I quirked an eyebrow. "Did you think I was flirting with that old man?"

She gave a deep sigh.

"Max Martin is not old. He's a fine specimen. Girls like you are often attracted to the older, dignified type of man."

"Eeeewww." I twisted my mouth in disgust. "Are you serious? I was just being polite, asking them how they liked their food. Isn't that part of the job?"

"Keeping the guests happy is the number one responsibility of every cruise ship employee," RK parroted. "As long as you were doing just that."

"I'm not looking for a sugar daddy, boss!" I tucked a strand of hair behind my ear. "Are we getting any lunch today?"

RK told me to follow her.

Ashley and the boys were already seated in a booth in the dining car. I asked RK if she was going to join us. Her face softened for an instant before setting into its usual grimace.

"Thanks, but I prefer a quiet lunch."

All the interns expelled a collective breath.

"Are you crazy?" Ashley hissed. "What if she'd said yes?"

"I was just being polite." I scooted in next to Jeong Soo. "Have you ordered the food yet? I'm starving."

"We're tasting everything on the menu," Mickey informed me. "RK's orders."

The food was delicious, especially the pasta in reindeer Bolognese sauce. Dani had been eating the same thing. She had been toying with it, actually, pushing the food around on her plate. At the time, I had thought there must have been something wrong with it. But the sauce was lip smacking, rivaling my grandma's.

Ashley and Mickey were mopping up the last bits of sauce with bread.

"You like this pasta, don't you?" I asked them. "Dani sent most of it back."

"Rich kids." Ashley clucked. "They have it so good. I bet Dani has never gone to bed hungry."

I put my hand on Ashley's knee under the table, offering silent support. RK might be running us ragged but at least we had plenty to eat.

Jeong Soo looked stricken. "My mom bakes chicken for me whenever the family's having noodles. I guess that makes me a spoilt brat."

"What kind of Korean doesn't like noodles?" Ashley laughed shrilly.

Mickey surprised me by volunteering some personal information.

"I'm a first generation immigrant. We're not rolling in money but there's enough to eat, thanks to the restaurant."

I tried to lighten the mood.

"So let's vote on these dishes, peeps. That's why RK ordered the whole menu for us, didn't she? Which one would you recommend to a guest?"

Jeong Soo voted for the salmon, Ashley chose the cod and Mickey and I thought the pasta was the best.

"What now?" I stifled a yawn. "Are we there yet?"

RK arrived before anyone could answer.

"Forty minutes to Denali, kids. Why don't you get some fresh air before it's time to disembark?"

I wasn't going to waste a minute. Ashley and I rushed to the viewing platform at the end of the dining car. The day had grown cooler. A couple was busy whispering sweet nothings to each other in a corner. We must've breached their privacy because they left soon after.

The train was crossing a bridge and I snuggled in my jacket, peering hundreds of feet down at the river rushing below. Ashley moved closer to me and I sensed someone else had joined us on the platform. It could have been any one of the dozens of passengers so I didn't turn around to check who it was. The newcomer started sniffling and broke into a sob I couldn't ignore.

"Dani!" I stared at the young girl. "Are you alright?"

Her eyes were red and her face was splotchy. Anyone could guess she had been crying her heart out. I was ready to bet my future tips on her grief being related to Edmund.

"What's the use?" Dani cried. "You can't help me. Nobody can."

Ashley rubbed her back and told her we could try.

"Is it boy trouble?" she asked. "They can be such jerks."

Dani burst into a fresh round of tears.

"Whatever's ailing you, it will pass." I was philosophical. "Things might look impossible right now but you need to breathe, Dani. Give it some time."

"You don't understand," Dani wailed. "Nothing's gonna bring him back."

Ashley's eyebrows shot up. I knew she'd tried her best. I gave a tiny shrug, letting her know I was equally clueless.

"Is this about Edmund?" I took the plunge. "You can be honest with me, Dani."

The poor girl's shoulders heaved as she wiped her nose and eyes with the back of her palm. I wished I could whip out a tissue and hand it to her. But I'm not that organized.

"My Dad can't know about this," Dani warned. "Promise me, Meg."

I gave her my word, trying my best to look solemn.

Dani told me she had overheard my conversation with Max. "You are right, Meg. Edmund was murdered."

Hadn't I been thinking the exact same thing? But hearing Dani say it out loud did a number on me. For the first time since that morning, I realized how ridiculous my thoughts were. Ashley must have thought the same. She was staring at Dani with a frown on her face but I suspected she might burst into laughter any moment.

"Who do you think did it?" she asked Dani.

"My father." Dani looked like her mind was made up.

"Are you crazy?" Ashley burst out. "Do you know what you're saying, little girl?"

Dani ran off without a word.

"Why did you do that?" I put a hand on my hip and confronted Ashley. "She was just beginning to talk."

"She was acting out."

"Whatever! I'm sure she has some valuable information about Edmund."

Ashley told me I was getting carried away.

"Break's over, Meg. Let's get back before the RK monster comes looking for us."

I told her I needed a minute. Ashley told me to focus on the important stuff and stomped off. It was her way of reminding me of the precarious status of my internship. She was right, of course. I was touched that she cared so much.

I grabbed the rails and watched an eagle circle the sky above me. And just when I was about to turn around and go back in, I spotted some movement on the shore. I leaned forward and peered at the rugged mountain, wishing I had a pair of binoculars.

"That's a bear!" I cried, jubilant. "I saw a bear."

Someone stepped on the platform and I whirled around, excited, thinking it was Ashley. It was Dani.

"Hey!" I tried to sound casual. "You just missed a bear."

Wildlife was the last thing on Dani's mind.

"Look, I'm sorry I walked away earlier. It's just … your friend wasn't very nice."

I defended Ashley.

"Some of us don't have fathers." I piled it on thick. "Do you know what I'd give to have one meal with my Dad?"

"I don't hate my Dad, Meg." Dani bit her lip. "But isn't he supposed to save lives?"

Did she really believe Max was responsible for Edmund's death?

"Calm down a bit," I told her. "And tell me everything from the beginning."

"He visited my father a lot," she began. "I saw them

arguing a few times."

I asked if she knew what they were talking about.

"I couldn't hear. But it was all very fishy."

How had she made the leap from a few heated conversations to murder? Suddenly, I realized Dani was grasping at straws. I had finally met one person who was actually sad about Edmund's death.

"This is all so sudden. You're in shock, Dani. Things will seem better tomorrow."

I was babbling the first thing that came to my mind. I was definitely not qualified to be a grief counselor.

"How?" Dani bawled. "Edmund won't be here tomorrow."

She bolted again, leaving me staring at her back. I realized something I should have understood long ago. Dani Martin was in love with Edmund Toole.

Chapter 12

Excitement ramped up as the train arrived at Denali station. I was charged with ensuring that everyone's baggage was collected and stacked together on a platform. The fresh air was rejuvenating, lifting my senses, banishing any thoughts of murder from my mind.

"Doesn't it smell heavenly?" Ashley flung her arms out, took deep breaths and stared up at the sky. "I wish I could bottle this, Meg."

RK made a 'chop-chop' motion with her hands, her way of telling us to get going. The luggage was loaded on a van and we started for our hotel. Actually, it was called a lodge, a smart way of charging atrocious amounts. I had noticed how some words like natural, historical or wilderness were used in abundance. But everyone's got a right to earn a living, I guess. My cynicism fled when the van drove through a massive pair of gates and parked before an impressive wood structure. A couple of bellboys arrived to get the luggage but we had strict instructions to help them. I lugged a battered suitcase with all my might, trying to drag it across the floor on a single wheel. Half way to the door, the handle broke and the bag snapped open.

A woman screamed and before I knew it, Jackie arrived and began moaning, flinging her arms around in despair.

"Close it now, you idiot," she hissed in my ear.

The brisk wind was doing a great job in picking up her clothing and blowing it around. I ran after lacy lingerie, grabbing it before the other guests saw it. At least that's what I thought Jackie's concern was.

RK arrived and of course she wasn't looking pleased. But she didn't berate me before Jackie.

"That handle looks like it was jury rigged. Not the girl's fault it broke."

Jackie wasn't going to take that lying down. She unleashed her fury on RK.

"Haven't you heard the customer's always right? What kind of training are they giving you these days?"

I tried to break up the situation before things went downhill.

"It's my fault, I apologize. All your belongings are back inside. No harm done."

Jackie didn't back down easily. She explained how my actions had embarrassed her. The whole world got a glimpse of her private things.

I'd noticed the cheap quality of her skivvies so I totally understood her. Thanks to my mother, I could spot an inferior piece of clothing a mile away. Jackie's wardrobe was stylish and she was always turned out well so she either wore hand-me-downs or bought used clothes from a consignment shop. People did a lot of strange things to keep up appearances.

RK impressed me by waving a magic wand and making the problem go away. Actually, she offered Jackic a $50 gift certificate for the spa on the Silver Queen.

"Not enough for a manicure!" Jackie made a parting shot before stalking off.

I wrapped my arms around the suitcase, pretending it was a teddy bear. It was a lot heavier than that. Mickey and Jeong Soo arrived to help. I set my ego aside and let them lug the hundred pound bag up the stairs.

The staff at the reception desk had already finished the check-in process. The tour group had ensconced themselves at the café and were rifling through menu cards.

"No rest for the wicked," Ashley muttered.

We spent the next thirty minutes serving coffee, tea and sodas. Most of them retired to their rooms to rest. Max took his son fishing.

RK summoned the interns for a powwow. I rubbed my aching back and tried to imagine what new chore she had for us now. Once again, she managed to surprise me.

"You can take a break now," she announced. "Meet me at the Wild Moose Restaurant at 1900 hrs for dinner." Her gaze swung toward me and I detected a hint of a smile. "That's 7 PM for you, Margaret."

I didn't even try to correct her. By this time, I knew she was just ribbing me.

Ashley and I both collapsed on our beds the moment we entered our rooms. The mattress was soft but firm. French doors opened on a deck with a million dollar view that made it worth every back breaking task I'd undertaken on this trip. I was torn between sitting out on deck or reclining on the bed inside. I chose the mattress, of course. We'd be back to our stamp sized cabin soon enough and I wanted to make the most of the luxury surrounding me.

I dressed simply for dinner and hoped I would be able to keep it down this time. The last embarrassing episode was fresh in my mind.

Ashley told me to chill, meaning she hadn't forgotten it either.

The dinner menu offered a lot of different choices and Ashley and I decided to split everything. I started with a cup of salmon chowder and gave it full points. Mickey had chosen yak quesadillas, a house specialty. The scallops and octopus were both local and turned out to be excellent.

Some of the tour group sat at a table adjoining us. I heard them talking about Edmund. The woman from earlier was defending him, stressing what a kind soul he was. I wondered why she had a soft spot for the dead man. One of the women had seen Edmund get into a fight with the jock. That led to more speculation.

"Must have been about Dani, of course," Jackie quipped. "Surely you noticed how she used to hang out with him?"

"Zack and Dani are seeing each other," his mom Ruth objected. "She's such a sweet girl."

"I'm not talking about Zack," Jackie corrected her. "Dani spent a lot of time at Edmund's house. I wonder Max or his wife didn't say anything."

One of the women told Jackie to stop talking in riddles.

"Dani had a massive crush on Edmund, of course!" She gleamed in triumph after making the incendiary statement. "I thought everyone knew that."

So my hunch was right. No wonder Dani was crying her eyes out for Edmund.

My dessert arrived, a fruit cobbler a la mode with handmade vanilla ice cream. I refused to taste the tiramisu Ashley ordered. It reminded me too much of my grandma Anna. She makes the best tiramisu on this planet, hands down.

The lodge had arranged a bonfire in the garden. We joined other groups and had a lot of fun, toasting marshmallows on the fire, singing camp songs. Dani sat away from Zack and he was trying to catch her eye, making puppy faces at her. So she wasn't speaking to him for some reason. Did it have anything to do with Edmund?

Max left the bonfire with his son in tow. I wondered if they were going to play video games in their room.

The tour group had opted for a wilderness tour before breakfast. I felt disoriented by the bright sunlight around us but my body was ready to call it quits. Ashley must have had the same thought too.

"Ready to turn in, Megs?" she stifled a yawn.

Jeong Soo was dozing with his head on Mickey's shoulder. I shook him awake. RK gave us an approving nod and warned us to be ready at 6 AM.

Max Martin met our group on the lodge steps.

"My room's been ransacked," he declared. "I think we better call security."

RK was right behind us so she took charge.

"Can you tell if anything is missing?" she probed. "Any valuables or electronic items?"

Max shook his head. "It's the principle. I've been robbed. The sanctity of my space has been sullied."

Was he really a doctor? He would've done great on the stage.

RK wanted to know if he had left any doors or windows open.

"You didn't leave any food out, did you?"

"What do you mean?" Max was irritable. "A bear came in and stole my stuff?"

RK reminded him we were in the lap of wilderness. It wasn't outside the realm of possibility.

"So we should go looking for a drunk bear then?" he snorted. "The mini bar's been broken into. All those snacks and tiny bottles? Gone!"

"You're too much, Megs!" Mickey howled with laughter.

I was so engrossed in hearing what Max had to say, I hadn't noticed when he and Jeong Soo had joined us.

"Is that where you scored our booze?" His eyes shone with admiration. "That's dope!"

I had a sneaky suspicion this wasn't going to turn out well for me.

"What's going on?" RK demanded. "Do you know anything about this?"

I reminded her we had been together the entire evening.

"You did leave to visit the powder room, Meg," Jeong Soo piped up. "You were gone thirteen minutes."

That wasn't enough time to walk across the lodge, go to the Martins' suite and rifle through their mini bar. But the powers that be had already made up their mind.

"Take us to your room," RK ordered. "Now!"

We made quite a procession. The door to my room was slightly ajar.

"Didn't you lock it behind you?" I asked Ashley.

She couldn't be sure.

RK stormed to my bed and stood before it, arms folded. A row of tiny bottles were arranged on my bed in concentric circles. Mickey let out a low whistle.

"That's a lot of booze for the four of us, Meg. And Jeong Soo is underage."

RK was trying hard to keep her cool. I knew she wouldn't rebuke me in front of Max. Surprisingly, he came to my rescue.

"Why don't you go back to your room, Sir?" RK cajoled. "I will talk to the management and make sure they refill your bar. And we are very sorry for the inconvenience."

"I'm sorry," I blurted out, remembering what the orientation manual had said.

We had to apologize to every irate customer, regardless of whose fault it was. In this case, Max Martin wasn't culpable but neither was I.

"It's okay, kid." He patted my shoulder. "I was young once."

He told RK to forget about the whole thing.

"Kids will be kids. They're just having some fun. I wouldn't have raised this ruckus if I'd realized what they were up to."

He gave me a broad wink.

"Next time, let me in on the plan."

RK pressed her lips into a thin line and assured him there wouldn't be a next time.

Max left with his kid and Mickey and Jeong Soo slipped out behind them. I prepared myself for housekeeping duty.

"Just when I think you're finally learning something …" RK slammed the door behind her.

I stood staring at it for what seemed like a lifetime. Ashley took me by the shoulders and turned me around.

"Enough is enough." Her eyes bore into mine. "You know this will only get worse."

The time had come to confront my bully.

"Mickey won't get away with this."

Chapter 13

I changed into my pajamas while Ashley went out to get some ice. Something wasn't right. I wracked my brains to figure out what was bothering me.

Ashley came in, holding a bucket of ice in the crook of one arm, a key card in another. My moment of clarity made a crash landing.

"How did Mickey get in here?"

"Say what?" Ashley frowned, looking puzzled.

"Unless he's a con artist who can pick a lock, he must have needed a key to get in here, Ash."

She stared at the bottles on my bed, her eyes growing wide as she caught on to me. Then her eyes flew to the deck.

"Did we leave that open? He must have come in from there."

"Shimmied up to the second floor like a monkey, you mean?" My voice dripped with sarcasm.

Ashley set the ice down, collapsed on her bed and sat

up on her elbows.

"Maybe the lock doesn't work. Is there a bolt on the door?" She must have finally sensed the hostility oozing out of my pores because her eyes clouded. "Wait, what are you saying, Megs?" She sat up, a blush coloring her cheeks. "You don't think I let him in?"

"Are you sure you didn't lend him our key?"

It wasn't my proudest moment but I had to be sure. Someone was definitely out to get me. What did I know about Ashley anyway? She and Mickey must have arrived on the ship at the same time. They could've struck a deal. Had Ashley been leading me on all this time? I wanted to think I wasn't so gullible but she was the only friendly face I'd encountered on the Silver Queen. Maybe it had been a ploy, acting like she was my friend but stabbing me in the back to get ahead on the leader board.

She must have read my mind. Again.

"Are you for reals?" She sprang up and rushed toward me. "You think I sold you out?"

I gave an emphatic nod, ready to tell her she was a snake in the grass.

The door flung open and Mickey and Jeong Soo came in, carrying armloads of snacks from the vending machine.

"Party time, sistas!" Mickey crowed. "I brought some soda for the kid."

"How dare you?" I put my hands on my hips and glared at him. "Didn't you just get me in trouble, again?"

Mickey told me to calm down. He hadn't meant any harm.

"Are you going to be a buzz kill now, Megs? I promise I won't do it again, okay?"

There was an honesty in his honey colored eyes that reached out to me. Against my better judgment, I decided to give Mickey a chance.

"This is your last warning." I summoned them in and told Jeong Soo to close the door. "You've poked the bear long enough, Mickey."

He didn't actually shake with fright but I think he got the message. I was tempted to regale him with how I'd planted my fists into some of the more colorful characters from my past but I held back. I'm actually a peace loving person. I only retaliate after the third or fourth blow.

The evening was fun. We swapped stories from our lives while the Lion King played on the TV. Ashley refused to make eye contact with me but when Jeong Soo and Mickey started singing 'Circle of Life', she joined in. We called it quits a few minutes after midnight.

I walked the guys out. Mickey told Jeong Soo to go on without him. I sucked in a breath, bracing myself. I half expected Mickey to yell 'gotcha' and tell me I was naïve but he surprised me. He cupped his hand around my chin and lifted it, forcing me to look into his eyes. I felt like I was drowning into an ocean of warm honey but I pulled myself up.

"Enough's enough, Meg." His voice was barely above a whisper. "I was a jerk. Can you please forgive me?"

Call me a fool but I believed him in that moment.

Mickey rubbed a strand of my hair in his hands. Then he gave me a broad wink and was gone in a flash. I stood rooted to the spot for a minute, wondering if I'd imagined the whole episode.

Ashley was under the covers, pretending to be asleep.

"I'm sorry, Ash." I got in my own bed and switched off the light. "What was I supposed to think?"

She didn't answer and I let her sleep on it.

Morning arrived soon enough. There was a loud banging on our door just before my alarm clock went off. I guess RK wasn't taking any chances. I shook Ashley awake and told her we had twenty minutes to get ready.

The group was assembled in the reception area of the lodge. Max looked alert but many of them were yawning or rubbing their eyes. RK clapped her hands and we made sure everyone had a hot drink of their choice. There were donuts and muffins to get us started although we would have a hot breakfast after coming back from our tour.

Mickey bumped his shoulder into mine when I was adding cream to my own coffee. We shared a secret smile. Ashley saw that and looked away.

Finally, after some lively discussion on who would sit where, the group was in the van and we set off into the wilderness. The lodge had supplied a tour guide. He kept up an animated account of the history of the park and everything we encountered. We stopped every five minutes to take pictures and just marvel at the beauty surrounding us. An hour later, we arrived at the entrance of a trail. Cecilia Pierce was the first to get off the bus to use the facilities and she roped Dani into going along with her.

Most of us were excited about hiking the alpine trail. Our guide assured us it was just over a mile and promised spectacular views of a lake.

Max placed his son on his shoulders and went after the guide, setting a brisk pace. Most of the others fell into groups and followed along at their own speed. The trail was well marked and ended in a loop so there was no chance of getting lost.

Ashley grabbed Jeong Soo's arm and plunged ahead, treading on RK's foot in her haste to get away from me. I decided to give her some space.

"What is this, Margaret?" RK fumed. "More teen drama?"

I reminded her I was well into my twenties. As expected, my response didn't impress her much. Using some common sense, I decided to give her a head start and lingered behind to closely observe a wild bush.

Cecilia had commandeered Mickey's arm, proceeding at a snail's pace. They turned around a bend and went out of sight. I realized the whole group had already gone ahead, except for Dani's boyfriend, the jock. He stood at the edge of a precipice, staring at the valley spread before us, his hands in his pockets.

"We better get going," I suggested. "No point in being separated from the group."

I was worried about coming face to face with a bear but of course I didn't tell him that. I expected a snarky response but he fell in step with me without a word. After remarking on the weather and telling some poor jokes, I'd had enough.

"Say, you had a fight with your girlfriend?"

"Dani's not my girlfriend," he shot back, turning red.

Then he corrected himself.

"I mean, she's not just my girlfriend, you know. I'm in love with her."

His statement didn't make much of a mark on me because my teens were still fresh in my memory. I had fallen in and out of love a million times when I was eighteen.

"So what's the problem, bud? It's all good."

His eyes filled with anguish and I realized his love was the unrequited kind.

"Dani thinks I'm an empty headed jock ..."

I almost said "Aren't you?" but then I pulled myself back just in time.

"She wants to be a doctor like her father, go to medical school. And I want to be a professional ball player."

So they had different career goals but did Dani return his feelings? I wasn't very clear on that.

"Why did you get into a fight with Edmund?" I confronted him. "Most girls don't like guys who use their fists."

He acted surprised, then denied it vehemently.

We had set a good pace and I almost walked into Cecilia, standing by the side of the road. Mickey was pouring sparkling water into a cup for her.

She took my arm and waved him away.

"I will walk with Megan now," she announced.

Zack and Mickey didn't waste a minute. They both bolted from the scene, leaving me alone with the old lady. She thrust her walking stick in my right hand and leaned heavily on my left. I didn't have to pretend to walk slowly.

"That boy is lying," she told me five steps later. "He and Edmund got into a big argument."

I stopped mid step, encouraging her to say more. It was also a ploy to catch my breath.

"What were they fighting about?"

"That Martin girl, of course." Cecilia shook her head, looking irked. "They didn't stop at words."

Was Edmund jealous of Zack's relationship with Dani? I found it hard to wrap my head around it, not because he was much older. I had seen a lot of girls have crushes on their teachers but Edmund hadn't seemed the type. I didn't feel good being unkind to a dead man but he wasn't exactly Liam Hemsworth, was he? Compared to Zack, he was an ogre. More importantly, he just didn't seem like the type. He was so shy he never spoke unless someone asked him a direct question.

"I find that hard to believe," I told Cecilia. "Edmund was a lamb."

"You don't know anything," she grumbled. "He put the fear of God in that poor boy. It just wasn't right."

I wanted to ask if she had actually witnessed this so called fight or if she was just spreading gossip. My guess was she didn't get around much with that injured hip. I imagined her sitting by a window all day, spying on people walking down the street.

"Doesn't matter now," I sighed. "Edmund's gone. He won't be getting into any fights again."

Cecilia's chest puffed up and her lips spread in a smile that didn't reach her eyes.

"Good riddance!" she thundered. "The neighborhood is much safer with that creep in his grave. He was insane!"

A gust whistled past my ear, making me shiver.

I'm not always a good judge of character but I was sure I was right about Edmund. He may have lost his cool with Zack but that didn't make him a bad guy. My gut still told me he was a victim.

Chapter 14

Ashley continued to ignore me the entire day. We had a big brunch at the lodge after coming back from the wilderness tour. Some of the tour group went on an ATV tour. Others chose to relax at the spa. I was at a loose end for a couple of hours and I made good use of them, going for a walk on my own on the lodge property. There were picture postcard views everywhere I looked. RK handed us our phones that afternoon so I took plenty of pictures. And I finally called home. Grandma was overjoyed to hear from me.

I poured out the whole story about Edmund.

"Am I being paranoid?" I asked her. "Why am I the only one who thinks there's something fishy about his death?"

Grandma's opinion was important. She's a celebrated amateur sleuth in our small town of Dolphin Bay. Grandma solved many murders that had stumped the local police force. What's more, she'd also figured out who killed my Grandpa John.

"Trust your instincts," she advised. "You're not fanciful by nature, Meg. It's possible you picked up something that makes you think that way."

"You mean bad vibes?"

"Not just vibes," Grandma explained. "Maybe some bits and pieces of conversation you heard or a person's body language. There are a lot of nonverbal cues a group of people can provide."

I suddenly felt vindicated. So I wasn't this crazy person who was imagining conspiracies everywhere. I wondered what she thought of all the pranks Mickey had played on me but I wisely decided against telling her any of that. She already worried too much. My Mom was in Los Angeles for some dubbing at her studio so I decided not to disturb her.

"It's so beautiful here, Grandma," I gushed. "And the food is amazing." I told her about the reindeer ragu and the bison burgers I had gorged on. "But I miss your cacio e pepe and your chicken parmesan."

The day turned a lot brighter after that. My smile didn't fade when it was time to serve coffee and snacks to our guests. Everyone was in high spirits after the day they had spent at Denali. The lodge was providing a special dinner with local food.

Mickey gave me a fist bump a couple of times but

didn't say much. Was he reconsidering our truce? I, on the other hand, was still trying to figure out if we'd had a moment. I so wanted to talk about it with Ashley who was not only older but more worldly wise when it came to guys. Hadn't Luca fallen under her spell just a few hours after she boarded the Silver Queen?

Dinner lasted two hours. It was a proper sit down affair which meant more work for us. My feet were aching by the time RK gave a nod and told us we could start on our own meal.

"We leave early tomorrow," she warned. "Make sure you don't stay up late tonight."

I took her advice and decided to turn in after our dinner. It was windy outside and the air was fragrant with the scent of wildflowers and all the greenery around us. The lodge garden beckoned and I went out for a quick stroll, breathing in the mountain air, unable to believe I was actually in Alaska. I wrapped my arms around myself, enjoying the chill. It made me feel so alive.

Dani darted around a corner, Zack following her. She was in tears. I felt sorry for the girl and almost went after them, wanting to make sure she was okay. Then

I held myself back. Why get in the middle of a lovers' tiff?

Ashley was asleep when I reached my room. I got into my jammies, hugged a family photo to my chest and burrowed under the duvet. I made sure I turned my back on her. Two could play the game.

The next day promised plenty of excitement. We were driving to Talkeetna on our way back to the Silver Queen. The plan was to spend the day in the quaint town, then board the train back to Anchorage. I nursed a giant mug of coffee in the van, admiring the scenery. Thankfully, the tour group hadn't lingered at the lodge, eager to reach a new destination.

RK offered a few choices for breakfast when we reached town. Max chose a café that offered a variety of options. I decided to try the local porridge made with barley and oats, topped with dried berries. Ashley ate a bagel with cream cheese and the local Alaska smoked salmon. Before I knew it, I had cut a piece of her bagel and popped it in my mouth. She stared at me, looking stunned. I realized my mistake.

"I'm sorry. I forgot you're mad at me."

A ghost of a smile lingered on her lips, just for a fraction of a second. She pushed the bagel toward me and got up to order something else. Why did she have to come back with avocado toast? I wanted to taste that too.

"This is like my Grandma's favorite breakfast," I told her. "She'll never forgive me if I don't taste this."

Ashley cut a good sized chunk for me and put it on a plate. She was calving like a 900 year old glacier and I was stoked. But I guessed she wasn't ready for a happy dance yet so I did it in my mind.

Max took his family for a helicopter tour of the mountain. The rest of the group wanted to go rafting on the river. It was a leisurely three hour ride that promised plenty of glimpses of wildlife. Cecilia Pierce opted out at the last minute.

She shuddered when she saw the raft bobbing on the water.

"I'm not getting on that."

Guess who RK picked to stay back with her?

"Would you like to visit the museum?" she asked the old woman. "Margaret can escort you there."

Cecilia Pierce waved them off with a frown, grumbling she didn't need a baby sitter.

"Why don't we go to the Visitor Center?" I suggested. "They will have ideas about what we can do for the next three hours."

Cecilia told me she wasn't interested in any dusty museum. We walked down the street for a block until she complained her hip was bothering her. I led her to an open air café with a good view of the mountain.

I fetched a dozen cups of tea and let her give me the third degree. There were many trips to the bathroom. I didn't appreciate all her questions about my life. Some of them were too intrusive and rude but my rebuffs didn't register with her. I heaved a sigh of relief when Max came back with his family.

The Martin kid wanted ice cream so Max handed me a bill and dispatched me to get some. I had never seen a fifty dollar bill in my life so I was a bit stunned. Dani accompanied me to the ice cream store.

"How was your trip?" I asked her. "Did you get really close to the mountain?"

She mumbled a response, staring at the ground.

"What's the matter, Dani? Why were you crying yesterday?"

I wasn't surprised when she turned around and started walking back to the café. I took her arm and gave her a minute. Pressure tactics weren't going to work here.

We started walking back to the ice cream store.

"Couples fight all the time," I consoled. "Everything will be fine, you'll see."

Her eyes flew to mine, her face white.

"Zack and I are not a couple, Meg. It's all in his head."

I hadn't seen that coming. Zack had sounded sincere when he spoke about his love for Dani. The fervor in his eyes had been real. Was he some kind of stalker?

"He got to you, didn't he?" Dani chuckled nervously. "Gave you some tall tale about how he'll do anything for me?"

"More or less," I nodded.

We reached the ice cream store and I ran my eyes

over the menu. Everything looked tempting. I asked the server for two ice cream sandwiches and told Dani to grab a table.

"He just won't let go." Dani started confiding in me after she demolished half the sandwich in two bites. "I'm not interested in getting serious with anyone," she sighed. "He won't back off. It's a kind of harassment, isn't it? I guess he wants me to feel guilty but I don't. I have goals!"

Dani swallowed a lump. She was talking a big game but I could see she was conflicted. I might have been the same in her place if a handsome guy like Zack followed me around, promising me the moon and the stars.

"Edmund warned him," she began and stopped midsentence.

It was clear she had worshipped Edmund Toole.

"Older men can be more persuasive," I began uncertainly. "It's easier to say no to someone your own age, isn't it?"

Dani listened intently, a puzzled frown on her face. Had she had an affair with Edmund? Although affair wasn't the right word in this situation.

"You're not eighteen yet, are you? Certain men are drawn to school girls …"

Dani swallowed the last bit of her ice cream and stared at me, dazed.

"Are you thinking there was something going on between us?" Her face broke into a smile. "He was my tutor, Meg. My math grades improved a lot, thanks to him."

Dani's eyes widened as she sang Edmund's praises. Apparently, he'd helped her a lot with her school work.

I placed another order for ice cream, choosing different flavors for everyone. I got a caramel swirl myself and added some walnuts and chocolate chips for my own version of turtle ice cream. Dani took one look at it and wanted the same.

We walked back to the café, carrying the thick paper trays with the ice cream cups. Fluffy white clouds marched across an azure sky and Denali loomed in the distance.

"You know who was sweet on Edmund?" Dani asked suddenly. "Jackie. She's obsessed with him."

Something about Jackie had always struck me as desperate so I wasn't surprised.

"He wasn't interested?"

"Edmund was a bit shy," Dani explained. "Jackie was coming on too strong, I think. She wanted him to ask her out on a date."

A man like Edmund would have shrunk back from a strong female.

"Did he refuse?" I asked.

Dani told me it had all been quite dramatic. Jackie threw a tantrum and accused Edmund of being impolite.

"She told him she didn't like being treated that way. She's a pushy woman, Meg. I thought Edmund would give in."

Jackie must have felt rejected. Of course, Edmund had a choice but a besotted woman wouldn't see that. I was a bit surprised that someone with a bold personality like Jackie would notice an introvert like Edmund.

"Jackie must've hated his guts," I murmured. "I'm

with Edmund on this one. He stayed strong and so should you, Dani. If you're not ready for a commitment, keep saying no. Zack will give up eventually."

Dani looked relieved. We reached the café and handed out the ice cream. Max told me to keep the change.

"But you gave me a fifty!"

His smile was magnetic. I pocketed the change and wondered about Jackie. Had she really given up on Edmund? She was a woman scorned. I knew that now. Had she unleashed her fury on poor Edmund Toole?

Chapter 15

Lunch in Talkeetna was a relaxed affair, for the guests, that is. I was starving by the time we got a chance to eat. It was almost three in the afternoon and everyone decided to go for the fish and chips. The beer batter was light and crunchy and the tartar sauce was piquant enough to cut the grease. The fish came from the local river and had been caught fresh that morning.

RK told us she had arranged a special dinner for the tour group back on the ship. She had given it a theme and was calling it Grandma's Specials. I wondered if lasagna would feature on it. Fresh seafood was fine but I was craving something hearty that did not come from the water.

The train to Anchorage arrived on time and RK ordered us to make sure everyone was comfortable. Ashley wasn't happy. The best views of Mount Denali could be seen fifteen minutes from Talkeetna. She wanted to be out on the viewing platform at that time.

"But guess what?" she grumbled. "We'll be busy pouring coffee."

The train slowed after a while so everyone could admire the view. Most passengers were already outside. We had to be satisfied with peering out of the glass windows.

"Maybe next time," I whispered to Ashley.

RK heard us and frowned. That meant she would give us a talk on how we always needed to have a smile on our faces, no matter how angry, irritated or sad we actually were.

The train arrived in Anchorage and we piled into a van that had been reserved for our group. We did a little drive through the city to look at some sights and then headed to the cruise terminal. The Silver Queen loomed ahead. I wasn't looking forward to my stamp sized cabin but I confess, the ship almost felt like home.

Max pulled me aside near the ramp. He was beginning to treat me like his personal drudge. I didn't mind, as long as he kept me flush.

"How can I help you, Max?" I beamed.

"You leave my Dani alone," he thundered. "Stop badgering her, okay? She's seventeen!"

That's what I got for being an agony aunt.

"No problemo!" I grinned from ear to ear.

I must have looked ridiculous but I was doing my best to act cool. Escaping RK wasn't that easy. She was everywhere! I saw her glaring at me from the corner of my eye and knew my moment of reckoning was coming.

Cecilia Pierce commandeered my help to climb the ramp. Luca stood at the top to welcome the passengers back to the ship, bearing a tray of champagne. Mickey materialized and handed a flute of bubbly to the old lady, getting a rare smile out of her. Ashley and Jeong Soo had already transported all the luggage. I jogged down the ramp for a last check, savoring the solid feel of land below my feet.

The ship's horn sounded, warning any stragglers to get aboard. I heard a shout and saw a family of six waving at me, running toward the ship. They made it with a second to spare. Time and tide wait for no man. Neither does a cruise ship.

RK summoned me to her office as expected. What she said was completely unexpected though.

"Was Max Martin threatening you?" She told me to

sit. "Don't be afraid to speak up."

I assured her there was no problem. She wasn't convinced.

"We see all kinds of passengers on a cruise." RK chose her words carefully. "Some, like Max Martin, are very rich. Regardless of personal wealth, they all feel entitled. But there's a fine line between good service and exploitation."

Can you blame me for staring at her wide eyed? I mean, this was the RK monster, the same woman who stressed we had to go above and beyond in taking care of the customers.

"You're not their slave," she continued. "Any … unreasonable demands … need not be met."

My mouth dropped open. Did RK think Max was asking for illicit favors? There was a warm heart under the rock hard veneer. No matter how dictatorial she acted, RK was looking out for us.

I leaned over the desk and shook her hand vigorously and kissed it. Or I thought of it anyway. Then I spoiled it all by blabbing like an idiot.

"He asked me to stay away from his daughter. He

thinks I'm a bad influence."

"Are you?" RK actually smiled.

This time, I knew enough to stay quiet.

She warned me to be on my best behavior at the welcome back dinner. I gave her my word and headed to my cabin, making good use of the thirty minute reprieve we had been granted. A power nap and hasty shower later, I headed toward the Queen's Grill, the specialty restaurant where the dinner for our tour group had been arranged.

I was a bit early. Ashley was already there, helping Luca set the tables. Mickey and Jeong Soo were just behind me.

"Don't we need to join these tables?" I had assumed the group would all sit together but Ashley told me they wanted to sit with their own families.

Max must have engineered this. The Martin family arrived and chose the most prominent table. Zack arrived with his parents and led them away from the Martins. Cecilia was next. She made a big fuss about where she wanted to sit. Ashley hastened to set a table for two by the window. When Jackie arrived, I presumed she would share a table with Cecilia. She paused before the old woman, seemed to hesitate, then walked a little further down the line and sat alone.

A procession of servers arrived, carrying appetizers that had been chosen from our group's favorites. The interns had been told to be on hand to make sure our guests didn't want for anything. We kind of split the tables between us by mutual consent. I wanted to stay away from the Martins so I gravitated toward Zack and his family. Cecilia was seated near them so she also became my responsibility.

The shrimp cocktail was pronounced just fresh enough and the goose liver pate excellent. Cheese soufflé came next.

"Would you like some company?" I asked Cecilia. "I can ask Jackie to come and sit here."

She looked horrified.

"Pass me the salt, girl," she ordered. "And leave me alone."

I offered to massage her feet after dinner. That seemed to mollify her. Zack's mother wanted more shrimp cocktail.

"It's all included, isn't it?" she wanted to confirm. "And I'm still waiting for the crab cakes."

"You can order as many appetizers or main courses as you want," I assured her.

I caught the eye of one of the servers and dispatched him to get her food.

Everyone was in a good mood, talking about the wonderful time we'd spent in Denali. Jackie stared out of the window, her gaze fixed on a distant point on the water. I felt sorry for her.

"Why is Jackie sitting in a corner by herself?" I asked Zack's mom Ruth. "I thought you were all friends."

She told me to sit beside her and started putting some sushi on a plate. I wasn't about to say no to a guest so I picked up a pair of chopsticks and mutely dunked the sushi in soy sauce. I could feel Mickey's gaze burning a hole in my back. But I wasn't worried because I had iron clad protection.

"Jackie's not our friend," Ruth hissed. "You don't know the whole story."

I told her I was all ears.

"She's the nanny."

The sushi stuck in my throat. It's a good thing that we both had our back to Jackie so she couldn't read my lips.

Ruth slapped me on the back, helping me dislodge the food. I didn't have to prompt her to explain what she meant.

"Jackie works as a nanny for our neighbors. This trip is like a present for five years of service."

"They sound generous," I croaked.

"It's just a few thousand dollars," she shrugged. "That's barely a thousand per year."

Nannies were definitely paid better than cruise ship interns. But apparently, they didn't mingle with their employers. I don't know how, but Zack's mother knew a lot about Jackie's life.

"Jackie was a bank clerk somewhere in Alabama," she volunteered. "She married a cashier who worked with her. But he must not have been good enough."

Jackie had started an affair with the manager. Her husband found out and couldn't bear the shock. He had committed suicide, leaving Jackie a young window.

"How did she end up in Colorado?" I asked.

"No idea!" Ruth shrugged. "Must've needed a change of scene."

Or she had killed her husband for his money and fled the scene. I kept this theory to myself.

"She must be mourning her husband," I clucked. "That's why she looks so sad."

A woman at the adjoining table heard us and leaned forward to offer her two cents. I shouldn't have been surprised because I had made no effort to lower my voice.

"Nothing of the sort."

She and Ruth exchanged a glance. Some silent signal passed between them and the woman continued. She hadn't been very vocal during the Denali trip so I was surprised she was suddenly taking an interest.

"Jackie's trying to snag herself a new husband."

"A rich husband," Ruth added. "Who can blame her,

poor girl! Changing diapers and running after spoilt brats must get old after some time."

Hadn't I signed up for a version of it? Except, in my case, I was going to see the world while doing it.

"Why do you think she was after Edmund?" The other woman's lip curled in a sneer.

I sat up in my seat. So Jackie had more than a few dates on her mind when she wanted Edmund to ask her out. This woman had goals.

The ladies told me how Jackie had been obsessed with Edmund. She had figured out that he was a good catch and must be sorry she missed a golden opportunity.

My woman scorned theory reared its head. How mad had Jackie been at Edmund? She must have pinned her hopes on marrying him. Had she wiped him out when they came crashing down?

Chapter 16

RK arrived before I could snag another piece of sushi with my chopsticks. I sprang up, almost upsetting my chair. Zack's mom was nice enough to make a big show of thanking me for my trouble.

"I've never had sushi in my life," she explained. "Meg was kind enough to demonstrate how to eat it."

I played along.

"You'll do fine. Remember, just a dab of wasabi. And don't forget the ginger. It's a palate cleanser."

RK fell for it and I heaved a silent sigh of relief. It was time for the main course and the procession of servers started again, holding aloft trays with plates containing dome shaped lids. The Martins had ordered rack of lamb and there was a round of applause as Max began carving it. Zack's family had chosen Beef Wellington. I picked up the sauce boat and went around the table, pouring gravy as needed.

Cecilia's dinner was the last to arrive. I saw her tapping her foot impatiently, playing with her napkin.

"Check on my dinner, Megan," she ordered. "I have been twiddling my thumbs for the past hour."

She had been scarfing down goose liver, caviar and deviled eggs but I didn't correct her. I spotted the server brandishing another steaming entrée and walked toward him.

"Let me get that," I offered. "Here you go." I set it before Cecilia with a flourish and lifted the dome shaped lid. "Looks like some kind of stew." I peered at the dark red sauce.

"It's Boof Burginyon," she smirked. "Julia Child's favorite dish."

"Friend of yours?" I asked, and was rewarded with an eye roll.

"You kids! Heathens is more like it. You know nothing about history."

"Relax!" I laughed. "Grandma told me all about her. We ate the best Boeuf Bourginion at a small bistro in Santa Monica. The chef there is a big fan of my mom's."

Cecilia buttered a roll and took a bite. Then she dug a spoon in her stew and leaned forward with a smile of anticipation. My job was done. I had barely turned around when a shrill scream pierced the air. Cecilia was thumping her fists on the table, yelling something I couldn't make sense of.

I was two feet away but RK reached her before I did. Tears were streaming down the old woman's eyes.

"Ice!" RK spat, pointing a finger at me. "Get ice."

She held a glass of water to Cecilia's lips and made her drink it. Then she almost stuffed a piece of bread in the poor woman's mouth. I just followed orders for the next few minutes, trying to figure out what happened.

"Are you trying to kill me?" Cecilia finally gasped. "You won't get away with this."

RK dipped her little finger in the dish of beef stew and dabbed it on her tongue. She began to fan her mouth. Then it was my turn. I knew I was walking into a trap but there was no other option. I ate a spoon of the stew and stars exploded before my eyes. The food was hotter than hot. I was sure it contained the heat of a hundred peppers. My throat burned, my eyes watered and snot streamed down my nose.

"This is not Bouef Bourginion!" I cried.

RK dispatched Mickey and Ashley to take Cecilia to the infirmary. The poor lady looked like she had the stuffing knocked out of her.

"What's the kitchen staff thinking?" I asked RK. "Is this some kind of joke?"

"That's exactly what I want to know." RK was grim. "Come to my office right now."

I got a proper dressing down. RK promised I would be taking a flight home this time.

"Tell me why I should wait till we reach Vancouver to send you home? Why shouldn't I let you off at the next port?"

I begged and pleaded until my throat was dry.

"Isn't it obvious? I'm being targeted, RK."

She hesitated for just a second, giving me the opening I needed.

"Give me some time," I urged. "I'll prove it."

She relented and gave me twenty four hours. Of course she didn't really do that.

"Get out my sight." RK began massaging her temples, refusing to listen to a single word I said.

I fled to the crew mess, determined to give Mickey a piece of my mind. Maybe I would rearrange his face a little. That fine, chiseled face with the saccharine smile.

Jeong Soo sat in the crew mess, gulping soft serve like there was no tomorrow. A bottle of chocolate syrup rested on the table. He squirted it on the frozen dessert after every two bites.

"How'd it go, Meg?" he asked, looking terrified.

It looked like he would break into hives any second. I snatched the bottle of syrup and put it away, asking him to slow down.

"What do you think happened?" I fumed, unleashing my angst on the poor kid. "She threw me out."

Ashley and Mickey arrived before he could respond.

"She's fine," Ashley assured me. "The doctor gave her a sedative and some kind of gel for her mouth. It should help with the sores."

Mickey brought over two cups of coffee and sat next

to Ashley.

"Poor woman! Can't say I blame her for all the fuss."

I banged on the table to get his attention.

"Hello! Is that all you have to say, you piece of scum?"

Mickey quirked an eyebrow, managing to look genuinely surprised.

"What's wrong, Meg? You don't look so good."

My chest heaved with effort as I tried to exhale. So he was going to deny everything.

"RK thinks Meg did it," Jeong Soo blurted out.

"And did you?" Mickey asked, his lips curving in a smile. "Zack might've been a better target for a prank like this."

"How dare you!" I sputtered. "This is not cool, Mickey. You just crossed the line."

The smile on his face froze.

"Are you accusing me, Meg?"

"Who else?" I spread my hands out wide. "All that talk of calling a truce and being friends was just nonsense, wasn't it? You wanted me to let my guard down so you could strike a final blow."

Ashley turned on Mickey.

"Is she right, dude? What have you done now?"

Jeong Soo was tapping his spoon on his bowl, making a jarring noise. It set my teeth on edge.

"You promised her, man." He looked so disappointed I realized how much he had idolized Mickey.

"Listen to me, Meg." Mickey placed both hands on the table. "Ashley, Jeong Soo." He made sure each one of us was looking at him. "I did not do this. I swear on my family's honor." He paused before continuing. "That means a lot where I come from."

He sounded sincere but he wasn't going to be asked to walk the plank any minute.

"Fool me once, shame on you. Fool me twice, thrice … I've lost count, Mickey."

He claimed he would never do anything to hurt a

passenger. That made me laugh.

"What about that soap in the drinks? Or the peanut butter on the sheets?"

It was like he was hearing about those things for the first time. Hadn't he owned up to all of it in Denali? Ashley spoke up before I did.

"Dude! You confessed! Jeong Soo was there too. You said you played all those pranks on Meg and promised you'd never do it again."

Mickey's eyes grew wide in alarm.

"I meant sending you on that train ride to White Pass, or giving you the wrong time for a meeting. I would never deliberately hurt a passenger."

"And you think I would?" I cried.

Mickey had believed I was responsible for doctoring the drinks. He claimed he didn't know anything about the soiled sheets.

I asked Jeong Soo to get pen and paper. He looked at me as if I was some Neanderthal and whipped out his phone. I began listing the different 'incidents' that had been blamed on me. The kid kept up with me, typing at an insane speed.

"Take a look at these." I told Mickey to check off the ones he was responsible for.

His eyes met mine and he obliged.

"That's it?" Ashley quizzed. "Are you sure you didn't do the rest? Maybe you have some accomplice?"

Mickey crossed his heart again and insisted he wasn't lying.

"There's a clear pattern here, Meg." Jeong Soo, ever the geek, told me that 30% of the crimes had not been committed by Mickey.

"But what does it mean?" I was bewildered. "I'm innocent, you guys. Believe me."

Mickey took the lead this time.

"There's mischief afoot. Someone's targeting the passengers."

"But why would they do that?" Ashley was as puzzled as I was. "We know how important customer satisfaction is for the cruise line. Aren't we taught to go above and beyond to please the guests?"

"An angry customer is bad for the cruise line," Jeong Soo echoed.

"I think we have a saboteur on board." Mickey's face was animated as he stared at me. "And you're just a pawn in the game, Megs."

He'd never called me that before.

Jeong Soo proposed going to RK. I opened my mouth to scoff at him but Mickey and Ashley agreed.

"Let's go now." Ashley scrambled from the booth. "Hopefully, she'll be in her office."

Five minutes later, I lifted my hand to knock on RK's door and turned around to flee. Ashley grabbed my arm and Mickey rapped his knuckles on the door. We trooped inside to find RK buried in a stack of files.

Mickey took the lead and gave a succinct account of the whole scam. I steeled myself to be ridiculed.

"Did you put them up to this?" RK asked me, her brow scrunched in thought.

I licked my dry lips and told her it was all true. If I was in her place, I would have pooh-poohed the idea too.

"Corporate espionage is not unheard of," she mused, leaning back in her chair. "Spreading discontent among the passengers can be very effective. They talk, you know? And word of mouth can make or break a brand."

Someone was deliberately trying to damage the cruise company, using me as a crutch. This wasn't the first time an opponent had underestimated me.

"How can we help?" I asked. "We need to trap this person red handed."

Jeong Soo shrank back but Ashley and Mickey nodded eagerly.

"We'll do whatever it takes to protect the passengers and the cruise company, Ma'am. This is a team effort now. Just give us our marching orders."

I thought he was being a pompous opportunist ass. One look at Ashley told me she though the same.

"Aren't you jumping the gun?" RK frowned. "We can't catch this traitor until we figure out who they are."

Jeong Soo thought we should call security.

"No need," I told them. "I have a lot of experience in this kind of stuff. My grandma's a famous amateur sleuth." A rookie police officer back home was my special friend but I left that part out.

I don't think RK heard me. Maybe she had a hearing problem. I considered suggesting she get her ears checked.

"Let's tackle this with a fresh mind." She dismissed us. "Meet me here at 7 AM sharp." Her face softened. "Breakfast is on me."

Luca was loitering outside our cabin. Ashley leapt into his arms, her eyes gleaming. I figured she wanted to share the whole drama with him.

"Don't be too late, Ash." I went into my cabin and climbed into my bunk, feeling the energy drain from my body.

The stakes had suddenly been raised and I realized my job wasn't the only thing on the line.

Chapter 17

The officers' mess lived up to its name with a more subdued atmosphere. Every person there seemed to stand up taller and didn't have a moment to spare.

There was an omelet station with fancy toppings like crab and smoked salmon. The bowl of cut fruit was full and the coffee was fresh. RK played the consummate host and made sure our plates were full.

"I gave it a lot of thought," she began, taking a sip of her Americano. "Frankly, it all seems fantastic this morning."

Ashley and Mickey looked disappointed but I had expected this. We didn't have any proof to back up our theory. RK echoed the same.

"I'm not dismissing your theory," she explained. "But I need something more solid." She leveled her eyes on Mickey. "Meet me in my office."

We thanked RK for her hospitality.

"It's part of your training," she shrugged. "The idea is to motivate you to work towards a higher position."

We headed to the crew mess to regroup.

"What do you think she wants with Mickey?" Ashley looked around as we entered the mess.

I had no idea. If I had to guess, she probably wanted him to keep an eye on me.

"What are we supposed to do now?" Jeong Soo asked. "I am scheduled to play video games with the Martin kid after breakfast."

The ship was going to be at sea for two days and the members of the tour group all wanted to do something different. After the previous night's incident, Cecilia wouldn't want me anywhere near her.

"We need a plan." Ashley stated the obvious, then looked at me. "How are we going to catch this saboteur?"

I don't know what I did to raise her expectations.

"Your guess is as good as mine." I gave a shrug and looked at Jeong Soo. "Put your mind to work, Junior."

We sat there, staring at each other, feeling clueless. I

don't know why but my mind was just blank at that point. I like to think I'm fearless but my usual bravado had deserted me.

Mickey arrived, looking solemn.

"Wow!" Ashley exclaimed. "You look like you just lost all your hopes and dreams, Mickey."

"Something like that," he muttered. "What's going on here?"

Jeong Soo brought him up to speed.

"Let's make a list of the different departments involved in these tasks," he began. "Nico the bartender was mixing the drinks at the Sail Away party, right?"

"Wait," I gasped. "You think Nico poured the soap in the drinks?"

Mickey told me Nico had been working for the cruise line for a long time and was a loyal employee.

"We need to question him, ask him if he saw anything unusual."

"You mean, did he notice someone who shouldn't

have been there?" I picked up on his line of thought. "I should talk to Edna too then. She's the one who handed me the housekeeping cart."

Ashley volunteered to talk to the kitchen staff.

"Luca works there so he can introduce me to his buddies."

I nodded. This was going to be easy.

"Let me talk to Edna."

Mickey offered to handle Nico.

"Why don't you report back to me?" Jeong Soo offered, trying to be helpful. "I can make a note of what each of you learned. We'll see if a pattern emerges."

Mickey told us our first order of the day was to serve our group at breakfast. We agreed to regroup at dinner, pretty sure we would be rushed off our feet for the rest of the day. Plus, RK would be keeping an eye on us.

Cecilia had chosen to have breakfast in her room. The others were busy planning their day. Zack sat at the farthest corner from Dani but he swung his eyes toward her every other minute. She was doing a great job of ignoring him.

Max wanted Eggs Benedict again and his wife chose the same. It was a local version with crab cakes and salmon and really crisp, rustic hash browns. I served them and also brought over a big fruit platter for the table. Dani and her brother wanted the pancake special. The lemon ricotta cakes with the fresh berry topping made my mouth water. Two rounds of coffee later, the group dispersed. Jackie went off without a word to anyone. Max was going to spend the morning catching up on some reading. He warned his family he didn't want to be disturbed.

Zack declared he was going to the climbing wall, making sure Dani heard him. I was sure she was going to give him a wide berth. Zack's parents headed to a Jazzercise class. RK wanted us to split up and shadow the group all day so one of us would be on hand to fulfill their slightest whim.

Mickey volunteered to take care of Cecilia. I went to the viewing deck to keep Jackie company. She wanted to be alone so I maintained some distance and decided to enjoy the view. The ship was making its way through some fjords. A glacier loomed in the distance and little chunks of ice floated around us in the water. A roaring sound could be heard and I watched with awe at the calving glacier, happy I was there to enjoy it. There was a round of spontaneous applause among the assembled passengers as people checked an item off their bucket list.

Jackie huddled in her jacket, looking morose. Her nose was pink and I figured she wouldn't last long in the freezing wind. I was right. She turned around ten minutes later and told me she was going back to her cabin.

"Can I get you something?" I asked. "Coffee, maybe? Or hot chocolate?"

"I think I'll take a nap now, Meg." She stifled a yawn. "I can summon my room steward if I need anything."

I hesitated. Did she want me to wait in the aisle outside her cabin?

"Why don't you take a break?" she smiled. "Put your feet up somewhere? I'll be fine."

The opportunity was too good to pass up. Maybe Jackie could empathize, being a notch above a maid herself.

"I'll bring you some snacks in an hour," I promised.

She insisted she was still full from her breakfast. I gave up. There's only so much you can do. I didn't want her to feel I was pestering her. The sky and the water around me had turned dark gray and a brisk wind picked up. I found it hard to believe it was mid-morning. The deck emptied soon as the temperature dropped. I decided to take advantage of the free hour to do some sleuthing.

The café on Deck 3 was famous for its special drinks. I asked for a Café Mocha with extra whipped cream and a dash of cinnamon and paid for it. The girl at the counter apologized for taking my money.

"We are not supposed to serve the crew here. The cruise line makes a lot of money from these drinks."

I assured her it was okay. The coffee was a special treat for someone.

"Edna's been very good to me," I explained. "She was so patient while I learned the ropes."

The girl knew Edna and felt even worse about charging me for the coffee. She packed a couple of big oatmeal raisin cookies in a bag and handed them to me.

"Tell Edna Talia says Hi. Now go!"

I made tracks to Housekeeping Central, hoping Edna was around. She was taking inventory. I handed her the coffee and the cookies and was rewarded with the hint of a smile.

"RK sent you here?"

"I have an hour to kill so I thought I'd help you."

She pointed at a stack of shelves piled floor to ceiling with bath towels.

"Count."

I got to work, pausing only when I'd finished a row.

"I didn't soil those sheets, you know."

Edna gave a shrug, broke a cookie in half and handed it to me. This was going to be harder than I thought.

"Did you see anyone else that day?"

She caught on immediately.

"Room stewards, maids, guests …" she spread her arms wide and lifted a shoulder in a shrug.

"You mean any of them could've gone into the rooms and messed them up?"

"Not without an access key," she said.

I slapped a hand on my forehead. Of course she was right. That meant it had to be one of the housekeeping staff.

"Would any of the maids do it?" I ventured.

As expected, Edna didn't respond. I knew when I was beaten so I said goodbye. My hour was up and I didn't trust Jackie. She would cry foul and complain I hadn't taken care of her needs.

"Nice cookies." Edna brushed the crumbs off her thin bosom. "Luca brought me some."

I flashed a quick smile and almost jogged down the corridor toward the elevator. I decided to get a peace offering for Jackie so I headed to the café and chose a selection of desserts for her to nosh on. My efforts paid off when she exclaimed in delight and told me she was a bit peckish.

The tour group came together for lunch. It was a leisurely affair that lasted two hours. Two hours too many for my poor feet. After they dispersed to various corners of the ship, we finally made our way to the crew mess to eat.

"How's poor Cecilia?" I asked Mickey.

She had sores on her tongue and could only manage cold soup and milkshakes. Mickey had talked the kitchen staff into making gazpacho for her.

There were carne asada tacos for lunch, in addition to the usual spread. I gave them the attention they deserved.

Ashley sat close to Luca again, clutching his hand while he fed her dimsum. I don't know he managed to align his breaks with ours.

"Edna speaks highly of you," I told him. "You work in housekeeping too?"

Luca gave a bow, followed by a smirk. Ashley answered for him.

"He tries to help where he can, Megs. Hard work never goes unrewarded, at least on a cruise ship. Right?" She turned to Luca for approbation.

He nodded and planted a kiss on her forehead.

It made sense as a strategy. Luca was making himself indispensable, paving the way for a quick rise through the ranks.

"What now?" I scraped the last bit of apple pie and pushed the plate away. "Do we have time for a nap?"

Everyone around us started laughing. Mickey's warm honey eyes crinkled at the corners as he offered me his hand, an indulgent smile lighting up his face.

"We, my dear Meg, have a towel animal folding class in five minutes."

Chapter 18

Sea days are fun for passengers but a real trial for the ship's crew. It was a few minutes past 11 PM when I finally had a free moment. The towel animal folding class had been harder than I expected. Max and his group had kept me on my toes during dinner. The only pleasant surprise came in RK's office at our daily meeting. Mickey's name was at the bottom of the leader board. I pinched myself to see if I was dreaming.

Jeong Soo led the pack again, followed by Ashley and yours truly had finally moved a spot up. It was no mean feat, as arduous as raising the Titanic. Neither RK nor Mickey explained how it had happened. Ashley had a theory. Mickey had been penalized for making my life hell.

We swapped notes but came up empty. None of us had learned anything new. We didn't have a single clue that could lead us to the saboteur.

A fiery sun hung in the sky, casting its shadow in the water. I thought of the evening I'd run into Edmund on deck, the last evening of his life. Had Max been responsible for his death? I stopped in my tracks, wondering where that thought had come from. Then

I tried to rationalize it.

Most of the group knew that Dani had spent a lot of time with Edmund. I barely needed a day to realize she had a massive crush on the man. Surely Max had been aware of it? But he was a busy doctor, I reasoned. He might spend a lot of time with his family on the cruise but his routine life must be very different. Had he known about his daughter's involvement with Edmund?

Hadn't someone mentioned that Max had been Edmund's doctor? He must have had a very fair idea of the man's state of mind. That also meant he could prescribe any medicine he wanted. What if Max had suspected Edmund was having an affair with Dani? Affair was actually not the right word.

I tried to remember any interaction between Max and Edmund. Trust was essential in a doctor patient relationship. Edmund would probably take any drugs Max handed him without question. Why had Max been confident that Edmund's death was natural?

I tried to reconcile the image of a generous family man who handed out twenty dollar tips with that of a cold blooded killer. My mind refused to believe Max was that kind of a monster. What would Grandma do in this situation?

The moment I thought of my Grandma Anna, my stomach gave a low growl. In our family, most problems are tackled with a cup of good coffee and a plate of cupcakes. I didn't have access to Grandma's cupcakes but a slice of hot, cheesy pizza sounded good to me. Fifteen minutes later, I sat at a window table in the café, staring reverently at the pepperoni pizza on my plate. With bated breath, I tore off a slice, satisfied with the long cheese pull. A ton of savory flavors exploded on my tongue and I closed my eyes for a moment, giving the pie full attention. By the third bite, I was completely hooked.

It was a while before I came up for air. My eyes met Zack's just as we both picked up the last slice on our plates. I gave him a mock salute and took a bite. He came over to my table.

"Mind if I join you?"

I motioned him to sit and tried to hide my disappointment. Who wants to be judged for wanting more pizza?

"I'm getting another pie." My eyes dared him to ridicule me.

"So am I," Zack smiled. "And breadsticks too."

He was a kid after my own heart. We walked to the counter and chose a pizza each, along with a plate of garlic bread sticks with extra marinara sauce.

"Couldn't sleep?" I asked after we'd each taken a bite.

He'd vouched for the spinach artichoke pizza studded with olives and dollops of ricotta cheese. It was a good choice.

"I was hoping Dani would agree to come for a walk with me," he confessed.

I gathered his efforts hadn't been fruitful. No wonder he was stuffing his face with pizza. His loss was my gain. What better time to make him talk? I think cheese has more power to loosen a person's tongue than wine. Believe me, I speak from experience.

"Why did you think there was something between Danica and Edmund?"

Zack didn't stop eating but his face turned red.

"Don't you trust her?" I needled.

"She was always there!" he grumbled. "At his house. What else was I supposed to think?"

His instincts had been right. Whether Edmund reciprocated them or not, Dani certainly had some feelings for him. He must have seemed so mature compared to Zack.

"Did Max know?" I asked. "How could he allow his daughter to hang out with an older man?"

Zack dunked a breadstick in the sauce and swirled it around. I let him gather his thoughts. When he finally spoke, his voice was laced with anger.

"Dr. Martin trusted Edmund. It was like he was sure he would never take advantage of Dani."

I tried to make sense of what he meant.

"Are you saying Max had some kind of hold over Edmund?"

Zack lost some of his bravado and looked like the teenage boy he was.

"I don't know, Meg. What does Dani see in him?"

That was one question I couldn't answer so I went

on the offensive before he turned any more maudlin.

"Does Max know you're harassing Dani?"

Zack hadn't seen that one coming. An array of emotions flitted across his face while he debated how to respond. Then his shoulders slumped in defeat.

"I love her so much," he pleaded. "We're the perfect couple, Meg. So good together. Why can't she see that?"

I told him he had to respect Dani's opinion.

"If she doesn't return your feelings, you'll have to accept it, Zack. You need to move on with your life."

He didn't want a life without Dani.

"I've planned everything." He was earnest. "We'll finish college first and then get married. Dani will go to medical school and I …"

I let him ramble because I didn't have the heart to stop him. The kid was obsessed. I wondered if Dani was safe from him. How far would he go to make her change her mind?

Then I remembered he had cooled his jets for a

while.

"What made you back off, Zack? Edmund warned you, didn't he?"

Zack's eyes filled up and a tear rolled down his cheek. He was slowly coming apart. I looked around, trying to spot how many people were around us. The café was deserted. A couple of kitchen staff were chatting with each other, kneading dough. Would they hear me if I cried for help?

"I did something terrible, Meg." Zack picked up a paper napkin and blew his nose. "Terrible. Dani's never gonna forgive me."

I didn't have to prompt him for the whole story. One day, after being rejected yet again, Zack had lost his cool. He threatened Dani and almost hurt her. Edmund had witnessed that and taken pictures.

"He blackmailed me, Meg." Zack straightened in his chair. "He was going to hand me over to the cops. My football career would've ended before it took off."

Since Zack was sitting before me, enjoying a luxury cruise in Alaska, Edmund hadn't gone to the police.

"It wasn't my proudest moment," Zack confessed. "But I would never hurt her, Meg. I love her too much."

I didn't know what had frightened him more, Edmund's threats or his own behavior. But Zack had backed off and left Dani alone for a while.

"And Max doesn't know any of this?" I mused. "You think he would've talked to your parents if he knew?"

Zack pointed out the obvious. He and his family were on vacation with the Martins. There was no way Max would allow that if he knew Zack had misbehaved with his daughter.

"Why did Edmund keep this from him?"

We could only speculate at this point. Zack was looking a bit worse for wear so I suggested dessert. That cheered him up. We filled our bowls with several scoops of ice cream and added hot fudge and sprinkles. I was looking around for whipped cream when he suddenly decided he wanted to go back to his room.

"Stay cool, kid." I bid him goodnight.

I'd barely finished half my sundae by the time I

reached my cabin. Ashley wasn't in so I walked a few doors down and peeped into the crew mess. My hunch was right. She sat opposite Luca, chewing on a French fry.

"Care for a cheeseburger?" Luca pointed at the tray of sliders on the table.

Very reluctantly, I told him I couldn't eat a bite more.

"Where are the guys?" I asked after Mickey and Jeong Soo.

It was past midnight so I hadn't really expected our teen prodigy to be awake. But I was surprised Mickey wasn't shooting the breeze with Ashley.

"Come and sit here, Megs." Ashley patted the spot next to her. "We need to talk."

My eyes were drooping but I obliged her, hoping she would be quick.

"I told Luca about our theory," she gushed.

She meant our mission to uncover the conspiracy against the cruise line and catch the saboteur red handed. But I didn't have the energy to correct her.

"He doesn't think there's another person trying to trap you."

I fought the cobwebs in my mind and tried to make sense of her words.

"You mean there is 'a' person?" I asked Luca.

He nodded but said nothing, prompting me to go on.

"But there's no saboteur?" I frowned.

"He means it's always been the same person trying to get you thrown off the ship," Ashley parroted. "Mickey!"

Luca stopped chomping on his burger and pinned me with his dark, brooding eyes.

"Mickey the villain here."

I stared back, unable to hide my disbelief. Had Mickey lied to my face?

"Wasn't I the one who brought up the conspiracy theory?" It sounded laughable to my own years.

"Not until Mickey put the idea in our heads." Ashley jogged my memory. "He was very clever, Meg. He owned up to the less nasty stuff so he could win our trust."

My head started pounding. I had already forgiven Mickey and brought him out of the dog house. Ashley was saying he had pulled a fast one on me again.

"All this for an internship?" I refused to believe her. "He's not hurting for money, Ash. It's not like he's homeless."

Luca finished his fries and began mopping the table with a tissue.

"Some people just mean." He gave a shrug. "You be careful, Meg. Don't believe a word he says."

Ashley bobbed her head, her eyes wide with fear. She was so besotted with Luca, she would go along with anything he said.

"Where's the proof?" I countered. "I need evidence before I can believe the worst of someone."

Ashley brought up my talk with Edna.

"She didn't see anyone suspicious, right? You should've asked her if she saw Mickey."

I begged for a timeout.

"I need to sleep on this, Ash."

My mind was in a whirl as I shuffled back to my cabin. Had Mickey lied to us again? Had he done all those nasty things just to win the internship prize or was there a more sinister purpose behind them?

I paused as a thought struck me. Had Mickey taken the internship to sabotage the cruise line?

Chapter 19

I woke up on the wrong side of my bunk the next morning. My mood didn't improve at breakfast. The scrambled eggs were dry, the coffee was burnt and they were out of donuts.

Mickey and Jeong Soo arrived, looking awfully chipper. They headed straight to the buffet.

"Slim pickings," I warned them.

Mickey came back with breakfast pizza, smoked salmon, bagels and a bowl of chopped fruit. Jeong Soo had a stack of pancakes topped with berry compote and a mountain of whipped cream.

"You don't fancy any of this?" Mickey schmeared his bagel with a generous amount of cream cheese and piled salmon on top. "What's wrong, Meg?"

I asked him about Nico. Mickey replied he hadn't learned anything new from the bartender.

"He really didn't see any suspicious character lurking around?"

"If you mean a man with a scraggly beard, a peg leg

and an eye patch, then the answer is no."

Jeong Soo found that funny and howled with laughter. I did the mature thing and walked out.

Max and his family sat in the café, making plans for the day. Tori, his wife, wanted them to participate in a trivia contest. The kid wanted to try the water slide. Dani wanted to sit by the pool and read a book.

I went through the motions, pouring coffee, fetching food, barely paying attention. My nerves were frazzled. Maybe I had taken on too much. I wasn't close to figuring out what had happened to Edmund. And Ashley had made me question the whole sabotage theory. The only way to discredit Mickey was to check up on him. I hoped I would run into Nico at one of the bars.

Cecilia arrived with Jackie, looking wan. She'd had a rough time and I felt sorry for her. But I decided to play it safe and stay away from her.

She held up a hand and waved me over. I couldn't ignore a direct summons.

"Get me an omelet with bacon and onions," she ordered imperiously. "And lots of cheese."

attention and some friends closer to her age.

We reached the spa and I handed my precious package to the super efficient girl at the desk. Cecilia was whisked away for her two hour treatment and I suddenly found myself with a lot of free time. I debated going back to the tour group to see if anyone needed anything. But they had three other interns to take care of them. My stomach growled, reminding me I had barely eaten any breakfast. I gave in to my hunger pangs and went in search of coffee.

The atrium was my first stop. Ashley had mentioned the bar in the atrium was the busiest since most people convened there multiple times a day. Three bartenders were busy tossing bottles in the air and mixing drinks. Unfortunately, Nico wasn't one of them. I talked to a Vietnamese guy at the Guest Services desk and got a list of all the bars from him.

At least I didn't have to scour the ship from top to bottom. Third time was the charm and I heaved a sigh of relief when I spotted Nico at a small kiosk in an alcove on the observation deck. Almost every lounger in the area was occupied by guests who were enjoying the natural beauty from a temperature controlled area. I wasn't sure Nico would remember me so I decided to order a drink.

I leaned against the counter and pasted a smile on my face.

"Ciao!" I tried to channelize my Mom but of course I didn't possess even half her charisma. "I need caffeine, lots of it."

Nico recommended a blended coffee drink and I went with it.

"Two shots of espresso, half a banana, four ounces of cream, chocolate syrup …" he chanted. "Wait a minute, I'm out of detergent."

"Ha, Ha!" I was a laughing stock. "Don't you believe I'm innocent?" I stuck my lip out in a pout. "I did not, I repeat, did not add soap to those drinks. I swear."

"I believe you." Nico drizzled chocolate syrup so it coated the walls of a tall glass and poured the frothy drink in it. "Whipped cream?"

I rolled my eyes. What kind of question was that?

"Who do you think did it then?" I put my elbows on the counter, clutched the thick straw and took a sip of the divine creation before me.

Nico told me he had mixed two hundred drinks in thirty minutes. He'd barely had a chance to look around. I couldn't blame him. After all, I hadn't felt a thing when the detergent sachets were planted in my pocket.

"Mickey helped you a lot, didn't he?"

"He was sucking up to your boss." Nico wiped the counter with a rag and frowned. "That Luca was a life saver though. We'd been prepping for the party all day with no break."

I remembered hiding behind the screen and stuffing myself with those appetizers. Of course, I didn't know who Luca was at that time.

"That food was a Godsend," I agreed. "I hadn't eaten a thing since breakfast."

Nico asked if we'd met before.

"You look familiar."

"I have a very common face," I replied and handed him a tenner.

"Meg Butler, you're anything but common." He told me the coffee was on the house.

"I wouldn't call it just coffee. It needs a fancy name like Coffee Goes Bananas or something."

I could hear him laughing all the way to the elevator. My two hours were almost up and I rushed to the spa, just in case Cecilia finished early. I sat there, cooling my jets, trying to gather my thoughts. How could a person move around undetected in a crowd? Were we dealing with a ghost?

Cecilia came out, ushered by a spa attendant. I was relieved to see a smile on her face.

"I could use a massage like that every day," she beamed. "Let's go eat something."

I suggested the high tea served in the dining room, thinking it would be the kind of posh thing she would enjoy. Cecilia agreed immediately. Half an hour later, we sat at a table for two near the window, watching the sun shine in a cloudless blue sky. She chose everything on the menu and insisted I join her.

There was champagne and an aromatic Darjeeling, with fresh scones and clotted cream, cucumber sandwiches and a variety of dainty desserts. Cecilia was partial to the chocolate éclairs and urged me to try one. I obliged readily because I never say no to chocolate.

The evening was a blur. Max had arranged for the group to have dinner at the chef's table. RK watched us with a hawk's eye as we served the group, taking care of everyone's whims. We helped serve twelve gourmet courses, each prettier than the first. The artistic plating and savory aromas made my mouth water.

The chef and his sous chefs arrived to take a bow. There was a round of applause as everyone thanked them for an unforgettable experience.

I saw the chef nod at Mickey so they already knew each other. I jabbed an elbow in his side and quirked an eyebrow, waiting for him to respond.

"Chef Lovely," he whispered. "He's a distant cousin from India. He visited us in Queens last year."

Alarm bells began to ring in my mind. Luca's words made sense now. Mickey had free access to the kitchen. If anyone asked him what he was doing there, he could always say he was meeting his cousin.

The dinner dragged on forever. Finally, Cecilia struggled to her feet and announced she'd had enough. RK tipped her head and I rushed to help the old lady.

"I'm fine, Megan," she trilled. "I've got my sea legs now."

The group dispersed an hour later and RK told us we could have dinner in the World Café that was open twenty four hours. I wanted to talk to Chef Lovely but hunger called. Jeong Soo challenged me to try something I'd never eaten before.

"Yak burgers!" he pointed at a sign on the buffet and rushed over. "Come on, Meg."

I took a bite to please him, just a bite, then moved on to my bowl of Pad Thai. There were four types of chicken wings and Ashley challenged Mickey to a wing eating contest. Things got ugly soon but neither was ready to give up, oblivious to the snot running down their noses. Jeong Soo and I stared at their sauce smeared faces and burst out laughing. I finally convinced them to call a truce.

"I need a gallon of ice cream after that!" Mickey complained, holding his stomach. "Where'd you learn to eat spicy food, Ash?"

The sky had darkened a bit, painted in a mosaic of red and orange. We sat there, ribbing each other, reluctant to call it a night. Jeong Soo and I got into a cake eating contest. He was no match for me.

Mickey proposed watching a movie under the stars. It was one of my favorite things to do on a cruise so I agreed readily. Jeong Soo and Ashley had never experienced it before so they didn't have to be convinced.

I needed to powder my nose so I took a timeout and promised the others I would catch up with them. A blast of cold air greeted me when I stepped out on the top deck. It was nice to be out in the fresh air after being cooped up inside all day. I could see the movie playing on the giant screen suspended in the sky. It was Casablanca, my mom's favorite. How many times had we watched it together, snuggled on the couch in our living room, drinking hot chocolate my grandma made? I couldn't believe it was barely a week since I'd said goodbye to my family.

If you'd told me six years ago that I'd be pining for my mommy at age twenty two, I'd have laughed in your face. That's because I didn't really have a family then. Getting adopted and eventually tracking down my birth mother had been a life changing experience.

I walked down the deck, lost in my thoughts, away

from the movie watchers. The crowd thinned as I walked aft and the area became more isolated. I passed a couple engrossed in the kind of things people in love do. I walked on to a zone with no deck chairs, put my hands on the railing and prepared to enjoy the view over the water. I allowed myself to relax and closed my eyes, trying to capture the moment for eternity. RK knew what she was doing when she took away our phones. I was actually living in the moment, rather than wasting my time taking pictures every two minutes.

The cold air and the gentle rolling of the ship were so relaxing, I almost dozed off. A hint of jasmine traveled over the breeze and I wondered if I was dreaming. I felt a tight grip on my ankles and before I knew it, I was vaulting over the wooden railing. My right hand slipped before I realized what had happened. I held on for dear life with my other hand and screamed in sheer terror. Fate must have been smiling on me because a pair of strong hands grabbed me again and lifted me up. I looked up into the wizened face of a deck hand and realized he had just saved my life.

Chapter 20

"Things are never that bad." The old sailor peered into my eyes, a kindly expression on his face.

He thought I'd been trying to commit suicide! I opened my mouth to protest but clammed up. Had someone really tried to get rid of me? It sounded ridiculous to my own ears. I pictured RK blaming me for making a fuss, creating more problems for the cruise line.

"Can we keep this between us?" I pleaded. "Please? It was an accident. I promise I'm not trying to hurt myself."

He gave a silent nod, gave me a pat on my arm and walked away. I looked around anxiously. Had anyone else spotted us? I thought I saw a familiar figure in the distance. I could have sworn it was Max Martin but he disappeared around a corner and went out of sight. My heart sped up. Why would Max try to hurt me? The only reason I could come up with was the obvious one. He'd killed Edmund and was after me now because I was snooping around.

My hand shook as I slowly made my way back to the elevators and I began to feel jittery. I thought of

Gino Mancini, my Grandma's beau. He would pour two fingers of brandy and make me drink them. It wasn't a bad idea.

The atrium was bustling with people. Nobody could have guessed it was past midnight, judging by the level of enthusiasm. I made my way to the bar and asked for a large brandy.

"You look very pale, Meg. Are you alright?"

I hadn't really looked at the bartender so I didn't realize it was Nico. I assured him I was fine.

I took my time with my drink. All kinds of thoughts were flying around in my mind. No matter how many theories I considered, I kept coming back to the notion that Edmund had been poisoned. Max Martin was best equipped to do it. Had he suspected Edmund of misbehaving with his daughter? That would be a strong motive.

Jackie was perched on a stool a few feet away. She looked wasted. I took my drink and pulled up a stool next to her.

"Hey!" She greeted me with a smile and tapped her empty glass. "Can you get me one more?"

I held up my hand to get Nico's attention and tipped my head toward her. He walked over with a bottle of tequila and poured a shot in a fresh glass. Jackie drained the glass and asked for one more.

"Do you have a man in your life?" she slurred.

I shook my head and smiled.

"Foot loose and fancy free, huh!" She gave a hiccup. "How old are you again? Sixteen?"

I told her I was twenty two. I looked young because I hadn't grown well.

"Malnutrition," I explained, telling her about my years as a foster child.

She put an arm around my shoulders and leaned close, blasting me with alcohol fumes.

"So you know what it's like? Not knowing where your next meal is coming from."

I liked to think my situation hadn't been quite that dire but who was I kidding? There were times when I'd gone to bed hungry. But I had worked hard to put my past behind me.

"You're doing good now, right?" I tried to shift her focus.

She couldn't deny her employers were generous. This cruise must have cost them a pretty packet.

"I had it good for a while," she sobbed. "But my husband committed suicide."

"So you had to take up a job again?" I prompted.

Jackie told me her husband had left her well off. She wanted a change of scene so she moved across states to her current job. One of her cousins had recommended her and it had worked out well.

"Do you ever think of marrying again?" I probed.

I wanted her to bring up Edmund on her own.

"That's the goal, isn't it?" she laughed. "Edmund was just right for me. He wouldn't have asked for much."

Had he ever reciprocated her interest? That was the big question here. I didn't have to try too hard. The alcohol had loosened Jackie's tongue and she was on a roll.

"He was just playing hard to get. That weirdo! I knew

he was going to cave sooner or later."

"How so?" I frowned.

Jackie told me Edmund had finally agreed to go on a date with her. It had started with dinner at the Queen's Grill restaurant on the ship. They had watched a show in the theater before he escorted her back to her room.

"When was this?" I wanted to be sure.

"The night before he …" Jackie slid a finger across her throat. "Who would've thought, huh? All that effort was for nothing."

I presumed she meant her attempts to seduce the poor man.

"Did he seem ill?" I watched her closely. "He took his last breath that night."

Jackie's gaze cleared all of a sudden and she sat up.

"He was perfectly fine, Meg. I think he enjoyed the date and was looking forward to the next one."

Edmund wasn't around to contradict her so I took this announcement with a pinch of salt. Jackie jumped down from her stool and bid me good night. I decided to stay on for a while. Nico came by to ask if I needed anything. I asked for a club soda with lime.

"Don't you have to get up early?" he fussed. "The ship docks in port around 7 AM. Your boss will expect you to be up and ready before that."

I had completely forgotten about the day in Sitka. The passengers would want to make the most of it. That meant we would be run ragged.

"I better go." I thanked Nico for the heads up. "Do you ever get off this ship?"

"Sometimes." Nico shrugged. "I'm too busy to notice."

I staggered to the elevator to go below decks. My eyes felt heavy and I was half asleep.

"Hi there." A voice startled me. "You're Mickey's friend, aren't you?"

I hadn't noticed the other person in the elevator until then. I almost didn't recognize him without his chef's whites.

I tried to clear the fog on my brain and flashed a smile.

"Mickey said you're his cousin from India."

"Something like that," he smiled. "I just got off duty. Do you wanna grab a bite?"

What does a gourmet chef eat at 1 AM in the morning, I wondered. There was one way to find out.

"Sure," I yawned. "Does it come with coffee?"

He laughed heartily.

"Coffee will keep you awake. I have just the thing for you."

I didn't think twice before following him into the bowels of the ship. We entered a small kitchen. The stainless steel counters looked sterile. Everything was so clean you could eat off the floor.

Lovely added a cup of basmati rice and a knob of butter to a rice cooker and switched it on. Then he poured milk into a saucepan and set it on the stove. I watched with fascination as he added some saffron strands, cardamom pods and ground turmeric to the milk. Then he grated in a good amount of nutmeg.

"Golden milk is a big craze," he smiled. "My Grandma made me drink this in the winter."

He strained the milk into a thick stoneware mug and set it before me. I blew on the frothy liquid and took a tentative sip. It was a bit spicy but it coated my throat like velvet.

Chef Lovely opened a couple of cans and set another pan on the stove. He drenched it with oil and added a bunch of spices. Crushed tomatoes and beans went in next.

"Indian food is hard to cook, isn't it?"

"Yes and no," he shrugged. "It uses the same spices that you find in many other cuisines – cloves, cinnamon, pepper, bay leaf – it's a matter of perception."

Something niggled my mind as he began to chop a fresh jalapeno pepper.

"Ghost chili!" I burst out. "Do you add ghost chili peppers to your food?"

Lovely's smile froze on his lips.

"I heard about what happened. Mickey told me you

had to take the blame for it."

He hadn't answered my question.

"So that ghost chili didn't come from the ship's kitchen?" I pressed.

Lovely added the jalapenos to the tomato and bean mixture and stirred it. The soup or curry or whatever it was had turned creamy before my eyes.

"We do have some on hand," he sighed. "Although we rarely use it, Meg. It's kept under lock and key."

I didn't understand why they needed to have such a dangerous substance on board if nobody used it. Lovely told me they never knew what a guest might want. Sometimes, they asked for a specific dish or wanted something cooked with a certain ingredient.

"Have you ever tasted it?"

"Once," Lovely laughed. "Once was more than enough. Now I just use it for my knee."

My mouth hung open. What did chili peppers have to do with his knee?

"It's a natural remedy for arthritis," he explained.

"You have to make a paste of oil and ground chili and apply it on the affected area."

It sounded too fantastic to my ears but Lovely assured me there was a science behind it.

"Peppers have capsaicin, see? And capsaicin is a known pain reliever."

"Is this one of your grandma's remedies too?"

"No way," he laughed, adding some cream to the pan. "One of the new hires told me about it. He made the paste and insisted I try it. Luca? Mickey knows him."

I thought the whole idea of anointing yourself with a hot pepper was too ridiculous for words. But I kept my thoughts to myself.

Lovely had been plating our food as we talked. He added a scoop of rice to the bean stew and placed a sprig of cilantro on top as a garnish. My first bite sent me into raptures.

"What is this called? It's the best meal I've had in a while and let me tell you, my grandma is an excellent cook."

"Bean stew and rice," he smiled. "It's what I grew up eating."

I pressed him to tell me the original ethnic name of the dish.

"*Rajma Chawal*," he obliged me, looking pleased. "Mickey was right. You're one heck of a girl."

I blushed furiously and took a few quick bites.

"Thanks for the delicious food, Chef. I better sleep for a couple of hours now."

Lovely gave me a thumbs up and began cleaning the counter. I guess I should've offered to help but I was so stuffed I wasn't really thinking. For the first time, Ashley was actually asleep in her bunk when I entered the cabin. I didn't bother to undress. My alarm would go off in a few hours and a busy day stretched ahead.

Jackie was on my mind as I drifted asleep. Why had her husband committed suicide? So Edmund was the second man of her acquaintance to die a premature death.

Chapter 21

I was dreaming of surfing at my favorite beach in Dolphin Bay when the alarm blared. Ashley was in the shower so I stayed put in my bunk, dreading the day ahead. I was no closer to finding the saboteur, nor had I made any progress in determining what had happened to Edmund. The cruise would end in a couple of days and Max and his group would leave without having to account for their crimes.

The interns sat at a table in the crew mess, having breakfast. I loaded my plate with two slices of quiche, biscuits and sausage gravy and joined the others. We had to meet RK in her office in thirty minutes.

"Do we have anything to report?" Mickey asked. "I talked to Nico, Meg. It was a waste of time. He knows nothing."

I confessed I hadn't fared any better. All I had managed to find out was how popular Luca had become in a short time.

"You chose a winner, Ash. Every person I talked to was singing Luca's praises."

She gave a shrug and tried hard not to smile. I think

she thought I was naïve.

"I'm not looking to marry the guy, Megs."

Mickey and Jeong Soo rolled their eyes in unison, clearly not interested in our girl talk. I ate a few hearty bites before tackling the hard truth.

"You know what this means, Mickey?"

He dug his fork in a sausage link and shook his head before popping it in his mouth.

"I was wrong."

A broad grin split his face.

"You're wrong about a lot of things, Meg. Can you be more specific?"

I told him there was no saboteur. Or if there was one, he was sitting right in front of me.

Jeong Soo turned red and opened his mouth to protest.

"Not you, sweetheart!" I patted his arm to reassure him. "I'm talking about Mickey."

His eyes bulged in disbelief and he swallowed a mouthful too quickly.

"Are we back to that again? I already owned up to what I did, Meg. And I apologized before RK. Why do you think I'm at the bottom of the leader board?"

I took the plunge and laid out Ashley's theory.

"You did that so you could shift attention from yourself, Mickey. How much more damage have you done while I was running around, trying to locate this spy?"

His mouth hardened and he looked away for a minute. I guess he was trying to think of a defense.

"You were present every time some mishap happened. I saw you near the drinks myself and your cousin Lovely knows where the ghost pepper is kept. He told me all about it." I couldn't draw a response out of him. "You've been laughing at me since day one!"

Mickey pushed away his plate and placed his palms on the table. He had our undivided attention.

"You're missing the obvious, Meg. Based on what you told us today, Luca was also present every time one of those mishaps occurred. He was near the drinks, he had gone to meet Edna that day and he obviously has access to the ghost pepper since he makes that chili paste for Lovely."

I heard Ashley gasp beside me but I ignored it. Mickey was manipulating me again.

"Are you willing to take this outlandish theory to RK?" I delivered the master stroke.

He agreed readily, managing to confuse me again. One of the girls from the guest services desk came in and told us we were wanted in the atrium.

"Your tour group's ready and RK's not looking happy."

We thanked her and ran down the I-95, bracing ourselves to face the boss. It was my fault, I guess. We had been so engrossed in bickering, none of us had looked at the time. The girl told us the ship had already docked and guests had begun to disembark. Max and his group would want to make the most of their few hours in Sitka.

RK's glare said it all. She fast tracked the whole getting off the ship process for the group and told us she would be at a local café if we needed anything.

Members of the group had chosen different activities which meant we had to split up. Zack went on a kayak ride and I was surprised when Dani joined him. Max was taking his wife and son on a private yacht to go whale watching. He insisted Jeong Soo go with them. Zack's parents and Cecilia were going to walk around the town while Jackie went on a hike in the local forest. Mickey joined her eagerly.

We had barely walked one block into town when Cecilia declared she had to rest. Coffee was ordered and Ashley and I stood by, ready to get whatever our guests wanted. Ruth told us we could walk around and see the sights.

"We'll be here for at least twenty minutes, right?" she asked Cecilia.

The old woman grunted and waved a hand in the air, dismissing us. I wasn't going to ask twice. Ashley and I were on the same page about this.

"Did you read what this guide says?" Ashley took rapid steps away from the café. "The only way to reach Sitka is by sea or air."

"Never mind that." Ever since Mickey had pointed the finger at Luca, my mind had been plagued with questions. Ashley was best equipped to answer them. "How well do you really know Luca? I mean, what do you know about him, Ash?"

Jagged grey mountains towered over us, juxtaposed against the dense forest. Sitka had a raw natural beauty that couldn't be ignored.

"I told you, Megs. We met at Orientation. He brought me coffee." She smiled at the memory. "He said I was pretty."

That's all? Ashley had fallen for a guy just because he paid her a compliment?

"You've seen him, haven't you?" she laughed. "A hot Italian guy was wooing me minutes after I set foot on the ship. I wasn't going to look the other way."

Something clicked in my mind. If Luca was our spy, he must've had some kind of plan. What if he targeted Ashley first? Then I came along, looking more gullible in my high heels, bumbling around with my complete lack of experience. No wonder he had chosen me to be his patsy.

"Is he nice to you?" I couldn't hide my concern. "You can never tell with these criminal types."

Ashley stopped pouring over the travel brochures and stopped in her tracks.

"You think Mickey could be right."

There's no shame in going to a higher power, especially when you need help.

"We are talking to RK as soon as we go back to the ship."

The twenty minutes were up so we headed to the café to see what Jackie and Cecilia wanted to do next. A couple of hours just flew by as we visited bears and eagles, checked out a cathedral and took in a museum. Then it was time for lunch.

RK had arranged to book a table for the whole group at a local crab restaurant. Max was his usual magnanimous self and asked us to join them. We sampled crab cocktail and Dungeness crab and I ate a big bowl of clam chowder. Mickey glanced my way a couple of times but I ignored him, reluctant to tell him he might be right.

Some of the group went back to the ship after lunch. We joined the others on a small hike through the forest and then it was time to say farewell to Sitka.

I thought we might get some spare time after going aboard but what did I know? The hike and fresh air had revived everyone's appetites. I think the average person eats four times more than usual on a cruise.

The Martins had managed to shop for an impressive amount of souvenirs and RK dispatched me to carry the items to their cabins. Jeong Soo and I hefted a dozen shopping bags each, realizing that scones and cucumber sandwiches were not in our immediate future.

My heart skipped a beat as we got off the elevator and headed to the cabins occupied by the tour group. Memories from that fateful day hit me like an avalanche and I tried to blot out the sight of Edmund lying dead in his cabin. I realized a few things as we made the long trek to the aft end of the deck. Max and family occupied two adjoining cabins. Edmund Toole had chosen the farthest one. He probably had an aft facing balcony. The others were somewhere in between.

What had Edmund done after his date with Jackie, I wondered. They had taken in a show after dinner and probably strolled around a bit after that. Three or four hours were enough to build up an appetite. Had he eaten something again?

I thought of the 24 hour restaurant and the pizza I had indulged in over there. Maybe Edmund had the same cravings. I discarded the idea at once. Dozens of people had eaten at the café that night and none of them had died. What if he had ordered room service? I felt overwhelmed by all the questions that had suddenly flooded my mind.

We dumped all the bags outside the stipulated cabins and walked back to the bank of elevators.

"Why don't you go on ahead?" I nudged Jeong Soo. "If anybody asks, I have a stomach ache."

Jeong Soo caught on. No wonder he was some kind of prodigy.

"I'll stall as much as I can, Meg. You be careful."

I ruffled his hair and told him to get lost, blowing him a kiss so he knew I was just kidding. The elevator doors opened and I stepped out, oblivious to where I was. A cold gust hit me in the face, carrying the tang of the sea and the scent of the forest along with it. I was on the top deck. The ship had just set sail and some people stood by the railing, waving at the shore.

The sky was dark and ominous and a wall of fog lay

ahead of us. My sixth sense made me look over my shoulder. People were heading toward the elevators, eager to head to some new activity now that the ship had left the shore. None of them gave me a second glance. Dismissing my fears as irrational, I braved the weather and marshaled my thoughts. I knew what I had to do next.

Chapter 22

I headed to the main kitchen, determined to find out if Edmund had ordered food. The only person I could think of who worked there was Luca. It was either ironic or very foolish that I was counting on him to help me out.

The whole area was a beehive of activity. Dozens of cooking stations stretched before me in either direction. People of different nationalities diced, chopped, sautéed and grilled a myriad of appetizing dishes in preparation for dinner. I spotted Luca immediately, pushing a trolley loaded with trays of fancy desserts, the kind they serve in layers in tiny glasses. I took a deep breath and marched in his direction.

"Not now, Meg." He cut me off before I could say anything. "I already got yelled at once today."

"Come on, Luca, this is important. It could be a matter of life and death."

He ignored me and rushed down the aisle toward the elevators, leaving me staring at his back. Undaunted,

I looked around in desperation, trying to spot some other familiar face. A tall figure stood at the far end, tossing vegetables in a frying pan. Lovely! I had completely forgotten about him.

I plunged ahead and smashed into a Vietnamese guy chopping a mountain of Napa cabbage. We both screamed. Several heads turned around to see what the commotion was. Thankfully, Lovely recognized me and came over to help.

"Meg! What are you doing here?"

"Can we talk?" I folded my hands and begged him, fluttering my eyelids a bit. It seemed to work in the old movies I watched with my mom.

He hesitated just a second.

"Sure. Follow me."

We entered a cramped office at the other end of the cavernous kitchen. A stack of files littered the table. I picked up a book of recipes and rifled through it.

"You have to follow these?" That didn't leave much room for creativity.

"Standardization is important in a professional

kitchen," Lovely explained. "Guests expect the same taste and portion size every time they order a dish."

I could tell I was trying his patience so I cut to the chase.

"How can you tell if someone from a particular cabin ordered room service?"

He didn't ask why which was good for both of us.

"It should be in the kitchen log, I guess. Do you know the date and room number?"

Lovely opened a spreadsheet on the desk computer and began scrolling through it. I needed a minute to remember the exact date. Lovely filtered the data to show all the relevant room service orders.

"I can tell you the deck number but I'm not sure of the room. It's an aft cabin."

After ten minutes of going through the data, I thought I might have given him the wrong date. We started from the top again and hit pay dirt.

"Six layer chocolate cake." Lovely pointed at an entry in the log. "Is that all?"

"Can you tell who delivered it?" I crossed my fingers and waited with bated breath.

Lovely wrote the name on a yellow sticky note and handed it to me. I was so overwhelmed, I gave him an impromptu hug, making him blush.

"Stay out of trouble, okay?" He cleared his throat.

I knew how pressed for time he was so I let him go. Next order of the day was to track down the person on the note. I had no idea how to do that. Maybe my fellow interns had some ideas. I considered going back to the dining room but the thought of running into RK held me back. The crew mess was a better alternative.

Ashley sat at our usual table with Mickey and Jeong Soo. I was relieved Luca wasn't around.

"We've been let off," Jeong Soo told me. "RK asked if you need to see the doctor."

"He handled it like a pro," Ashley beamed. "Described how you were beset with cramps. The monster bought it, Meg."

Mickey was eating meatloaf with extra ketchup and mashed potatoes. My stomach grumbled and I decided to address my hunger pangs first. One of the staff was just placing a roast chicken on the counter. I carved myself a drumstick and thigh and debated between mashed and scalloped potatoes. Then I added some green beans and a chunk of meat loaf, just in case.

The food was delicious and I gave it full justice, listening to the others ramble for some time. I pulled the sticky note Chef Lovely had given me and handed it to Ashley.

"Do you know this guy? Must be a waiter or steward or whatever they call them."

Ashley offered to ask Luca. I snatched the paper from her hands and waved it before Mickey. Did he need an invitation?

"Sorry, Meg. Why is he important?"

Jeong Soo saved the day. I don't know how he had run into the guy but he appeared to know him well.

"Li's relatives own my favorite restaurant in Chinatown," he told us. "He visited San Francisco one summer when he was seven."

Any other time, I would've loved to listen to Li's life

story but the clock was ticking. I hated to interrupt Jeong Soo since he rarely spoke much.

"Do you know where to find him?"

He had a few ideas so I skipped dessert and went along. Mickey and Ashley offered to stay put in the crew mess in case Li turned up there. I don't know how they were going to recognize him but I gave them the benefit of the doubt, hoping they would figure it out. I suspected Ashley was waiting for Luca but didn't want to admit it. We didn't have any proof against Luca yet so I decided to pick my battles.

Jeong Soo led me on a nice tour of the ship. We finally located Li on Deck 4. He was on duty but was willing to talk to us.

"The dinner rush is over. People won't order anything for a couple of hours."

I told him about the kitchen log. He was blessed with a sharp memory but he delivered food to dozens of cabins during a shift. I asked if he had encountered anyone on the way.

"How many days ago?" he asked again.

I tried to count the days on my fingers. Truth is, I

wasn't sure myself.

"The kitchen sent it out and you are listed as the server."

Li gave a shrug and promised to think about it. I couldn't hold him back much longer since he was working a shift.

"Can I get you anything?" I asked, thanking him for his help.

He asked when I was going to play the next prank. I made a big effort to smile and told him to wait and watch. Li was going to lose whatever money he had put in the betting pool.

Jeong Soo had a bright idea as we stood in front of the elevators.

"Why don't we trace the route from the kitchen to Edmund's room?" he asked.

At this point, I was ready to try anything. Jeong Soo sensed my reluctance and explained what he was thinking.

"We can see where the food might be left unguarded."

I humored him and we began our journey in the kitchen. Jeong Soo took some notes and I presumed he would give me a report later. We walked right up to the aft cabin that had belonged to Edmund. Something about it struck me for the first time. The entire tour group's cabins came before his. That meant anyone could have stepped out and tampered with the chocolate cake. But who hated Edmund enough to do that? None of them seemed to have a strong enough motive to hurt him. Or I hadn't discovered it yet.

For the first time, I wondered if Max was right about Edmund's death being natural. Everything I had discovered until now indicated I was on a wild goose chase. Jeong Soo interrupted my thoughts and tapped the pad he had been writing on.

"There are a dozen places someone might have tampered with the food, Meg. That's too many variables."

"I don't know where I got this crazy idea, Jeong Soo. You must be laughing at my stupidity."

He rewarded me with a wide grin.

"On the contrary, Meg. This allows us to narrow our

scope. Why would a random stranger poison Edmund? The tour group was the only one in close contact with him. And their cabins are located right before his."

I felt a burst of energy course through my body. Jeong Soo had managed to revive my flagging spirit.

"You think so too?"

Proving it was going to be a Herculean task.

We trudged back to the crew mess. Mickey and Ashley were eating pie.

"You didn't have to wait up." I sighed deeply and sat down. The day was catching up with me.

"RK was here," Mickey informed us. "She wants an update, Meg."

"Now?" I glanced at my watch. "It's past midnight."

I dragged myself to my feet and prepared myself to face the boss. We trooped down the I-95 single file and huddled outside the door marked 'Training Manager'.

RK answered my knock in a sharp tone. I wondered

about the source of her unlimited energy.

"Have you seen the doctor?" she asked me first. "Maybe you shouldn't go on shore tomorrow. You can help with inventory."

Juneau was calling my name so I assured her I was fine. A bit of Pepto had been enough to curb my stomach pains.

RK rubbed her eyes and leaned back in her seat, her eyes roving over each of us.

"Do you have any update on the saboteur?"

Mickey looked at me and tipped his head. He wanted me to take the first bullet.

I started outlining my efforts, deliberating over every little detail. RK told me to speed things up.

"Spit it out, Meg."

I risked Ashley's wrath and blurted out my suspicions about Luca. RK's face was set in a mask. I expected her to ridicule my theory.

"Things have escalated," she sighed. "There have been a flood of incidents across the ship, 40% more than usual. Management is looking into it."

I held my breath, wondering if she was going to throw me under the bus after all.

"Here's what I'm going to do," she declared. "I'll ask security to look into this Luca Fontana, dig up his background. We'll take it from there."

Ashley was the first one out of the door. I had a nagging suspicion she would go in search of Luca. A sudden thought made me gasp. Could Ashley be involved in all the pranks? She was in a perfect position to keep tabs on me, being my roomie. How many personal secrets had I confided in her?

The phone on RK's desk trilled and she answered it with a frown. I realized the others had left while I was lost in my thoughts. Would she mind if I slipped away or did I need to take her permission? It seemed like she was just beginning to be civil to me and I didn't want to antagonize her. My hesitation cost me.

"Hold on a minute, Meg." RK held up a finger while she hung up the phone. "I need a favor."

I stood up straighter and asked how I could help.

"Cecilia Pierce wants to go to the casino. She needs

company."

"Don't worry," I assured her, trying to keep my eyes open. "I'll take care of her."

She looked relieved. I welcomed the opportunity to spend time with someone from the tour group. It was one way I could learn more about Edmund.

Chapter 23

Cecilia Pierce wore a sparkly cocktail dress for her jaunt to the casino. She greeted me like a long lost friend, rubbing her hands with glee.

"Let's win some money!"

Her eyes gleamed with excitement. Clearly, she'd napped for a few hours and was rearing to go now.

"I thought you didn't like to gamble?"

Cecilia moved fast inspite of her cane. Apparently, her hip wasn't bothering her that night.

"When did I say that?" She shook her head. "I hate bingo but I like casinos. My husband and I spent a week in Vegas every winter."

I didn't really care. All I could think about was a cup of steaming coffee. Did they serve that in the casino?

Cecilia pulled out a bundle of pennies from her cavernous handbag and settled down to play the slots. I was dispatched to get a Shirley Temple for her. I stood at the bar, yawning my head off. The bartender took pity on me and poured me a cup of coffee.

"Thank you so much!" I cupped my hands around the stoneware mug. "I'm an intern. My name is …"

"Meg," he winked. "My money's on you, girl. You better beat the odds."

I rewarded him with a wide grin. How big was this betting pool anyway and how many people were taking a chance on my messing everything up?

"You betcha!"

I played a game of patience while Cecilia played the slots. It was agonizing to watch her put the pennies in the slot machines one by one and pull the handle, then do it all over again. She moved around the casino floor, trying her luck at a dozen machines. I was asleep on my feet when she declared she was done.

We trudged back to her cabin and I finally bid her goodnight. I sleepwalked my way to the elevator and stumbled into Li. He was just getting off a shift.

"There's a party on the crew deck," he informed me. "Wanna come?"

I told him I had to be up in four hours.

"So what?" he laughed. "You work hard all day. Now it's time to chill."

It was a tempting offer but I asked him for a rain check. He didn't know what that was so I spent the next five minutes explaining it. The elevator had spit us out near the atrium. Taking my chances, I asked him if he'd remembered anything about that night.

"Did you stop anywhere on the way? I mean, was this chocolate cake the only thing you took from the kitchen to that cabin?"

The mention of cake jogged his memory.

"Carrot cake," he frowned. "Chef Henri, the pastry chef, makes very good carrot cake."

Li had been working without a break and had been tempted to take a bite. He didn't remember anything beyond that. We parted ways and I headed to the kitchens, crossing my fingers and hoping my friendly neighborhood chef would be on hand to help.

Lovely sat on a table in his galley, eating beans and rice. His face creased into a smile when he saw me.

"Mickey says you're sweet on me."

I blushed furiously. This kind of blatant flirting wasn't my cup of tea.

"I need your help," I spluttered. "It's okay if you're busy. I don't want to disturb you."

He pointed a fork at his bowl and gave a shrug.

"I'm never too busy for you, Meg."

"Can we look at the kitchen log again?"

He obliged me without asking any questions. This time, I had an idea what I was looking for. The carrot cake wasn't hard to find and my hunch paid off when I discovered where it had been delivered. It was to Jackie's room.

I thanked Lovely and gave a deep yawn, determined to go straight to my cabin this time. He asked if I was hungry.

"I could eat." I gave a shrug. "But I also need to sleep. We're in Juneau tomorrow."

He told me to wait and pulled out a cheesecake from one of the refrigerators. Cutting a generous slice, he put it on a plate and wrapped it in foil. I suddenly felt ravenous.

"You're awesome!" I thanked him and headed back to my cabin, clutching the cake to my chest.

Ashley wasn't in yet but I was too exhausted to speculate about her whereabouts. I scrambled to my bunk and enjoyed my treat, falling asleep with the fork in my hand and the tiny paper plate on my chest.

My tiny alarm clock did its thing a few hours later. I was going to chuck it in the ocean one of these days. I sat up in my bunk, taking care not to bump my head on the roof of the cabin and peeped down. There was a body huddled under the blankets so Ashley was asleep. I suddenly felt a flash of irritation, feeling she was being disloyal by spending so much time with Luca. But then, we had met only a few days ago and she didn't owe me anything.

The hot shower woke me up. My mind was crystal clear as I wrapped a towel around my body and a few snatches of some forgotten conversation came flooding in. Ruth Heinzman had mentioned how Edmund had brushed Jackie off, telling her he wasn't interested in her. Why had he taken her to dinner then?

I headed to the crew mess, feeling ravenous. Chocolate chip pancakes were on my mind and they were the first item I saw on the buffet. Loading my plate with a good sized stack, crispy bacon and some cheesy scrambled eggs, I looked around for a table. Jeong Soo was engrossed in writing something in a large notebook, his dark hair falling over his eyes. He lifted a hand to greet me but barely said a word.

"Is that homework?" I joked.

He closed the book with a snap and picked up a tall glass of chocolate milk.

"Trying to get a head start," he explained. "Dr. Martin says good knowledge of the human anatomy is critical for a surgeon."

I let him ramble on, devoting myself to the excellent hot cakes. I was so engrossed I didn't notice Li until he sat down next to me and asked me to scoot over.

"Good Morning, Meg! Are you free tonight?"

I couldn't stop thinking of the carrot cake.

"The woman you delivered the cake to," I replied. "Did she come out of her cabin to get it from you?"

Li frowned before his face settled into a resigned expression.

"Of course not! It's called room service for a reason."

I asked him the same question again, knowing he might just get up and leave.

"No, Meg!" He shook his head. "I went into the cabin, placed the carrot cake the lady ordered on the table beside the couch and went out."

What had happened to the cart while he went in? Li told me the cart had remained in the aisle since he was just delivering a tiny plate.

Mickey arrived, pink from a fresh shower, smelling of Zest soap.

"The pancakes any good?" he greeted me with a smile. "Sugar and coffee is exactly what I need."

Ashley shuffled in, her eyes heavy with sleep, still in her pajamas.

"Why didn't you wake me, Megs?" Her face settled in a pout. "Now I have to choose between a shower and breakfast."

She grabbed an apple from a bowl, picked up a couple of strips of bacon and went out, munching it noisily.

After a quick meeting with RK, we joined our tour group in the dining room. They had just finished breakfast and were eager to get off the ship. Cecilia was bundled up in warm clothes, tapping her cane impatiently. I was relieved when she summoned Mickey and told him to stay close.

Juneau was rugged and beautiful. Overcast skies, a light drizzle and a bitter wind made it more so. Max wanted to take his family whale watching. But Dani wanted to ride the tramway and she prevailed. There was a long line for tickets so the interns were dispatched to get coffee. I was surprised when Jackie decided to accompany me.

"I'd rather walk around," she confided. "This might be my first and last visit to Juneau."

"You're young." She probably needed some validation. "Plenty of time to come back."

We spotted a café and went in. I saw Jackie eyeing the display case and thought it was now or never.

"You like cake, huh?"

"Who doesn't?" Jackie's response was automatic.

"What's your favorite?" I pressed. "Chocolate or carrot?"

"Oh, carrot cake!" She played into my hands, patting her stomach. "I can eat carrot cake every day of the year."

"And night?" I prompted. "I think dessert always tastes better at night." I laughed for extra effect.

Jackie rattled off our drinks order and turned around.

"What were you saying?"

"Did you order carrot cake after you got back from the show?" I took the plunge.

Her eyes widened. I wouldn't have to explain which day I meant.

"Have you been talking to my steward? It was such a sweet surprise." She laughed at the pun. "Tell him I'm going to give a very generous tip."

I had seen the kitchen log myself so I knew someone had placed that order. Was Jackie lying to my face?

I went over her possible motive as we took the drinks back to the group. Was her ego that fragile? Killing someone just because they didn't want to date you was a bit of a stretch. My head was beginning to pound and it was our turn to board the tram. Thoughts of Edmund flew out of my head when the car started ascending the mountain. We stepped out after a short but exhilarating six minutes, 1800 feet above the sea.

"That's us." Mickey pointed at a tiny cruise ship moored at the dock. "You ready for a hike, Meg?"

The ladies wanted to shop first but Max convinced them otherwise. The group split up and this time, Ashley and I tagged along with the Martin family. The sky had cleared and a couple of hours passed walking under towering trees among wildflowers, with gorgeous views of the water and mountain peaks surrounding us.

After a quick lunch, we took a trip to the Mendenhall Glacier. I saw Dani talk to Zack once or twice so they had apparently reached a truce. Max Martin seemed oblivious of Zack's presence. The day passed quickly and it was time to return to the ship. I didn't have any bittersweet feelings like Jackie because I presumed I would be back in Juneau several times that summer.

RK stood next to the cruise director to welcome the guests. She crooked a finger when she saw me and summoned us to her office.

Mickey put a hand on my shoulder and squeezed it. Was I going to be exonerated at last?

"You may be right, Meg," she admitted. "Luca worked for a rival cruise line before getting a job here."

"Is that unusual?" Ashley asked. "Maybe his contract ended and he got a new one here."

"That is possible," RK agreed. "That's why I asked security to dig deeper into his movements. They are going to question him soon."

I saw our case collapsing before it got off the ground. Luca could easily deny everything. The most the cruise line could do was fire him. That wouldn't be enough to clear my name.

"We need to catch him red handed, RK."

All eyes turned toward me. I didn't think I had said anything earth shattering.

"I have a plan."

RK's expression told me she was skeptical but I had nothing to lose.

"Today's formal night," I continued. "I bet a lot of people get their clothes pressed for the event?"

RK gave a grudging nod.

"People in the suites don't mind shelling out a few extra bucks. What's your point?"

I thought on my feet. What if Luca was asked to deliver laundry to a few people?

"We can tell him the guest is very finicky, emphasize how important it is."

"She wants to dangle some bait before him," Jeong Soo pitched in.

I flashed him a grateful smile and waited for RK's response.

"What do you think he'll do?" she mused.

"Tomorrow's the last day of the cruise," I reminded her. "I think Luca must be getting desperate. We'll follow him and see what he does."

Ashley whirled around, her hands on her hips.

"What if he does nothing? Will you stop this ridiculous witch hunt, Megs?"

I knew the whole plan was a gamble so I said nothing.

RK thought for a minute and chose Mickey and Jeong Soo for the task. The kid asked for his phone so he could take pictures.

"You still don't trust me?" I asked RK.

"I don't want him to suspect anything," she replied, warning Ashley to stay away too. "Why don't you girls dress up for tonight? Wear something nice."

My mouth dropped open when she handed us two passes for the steam and sauna rooms at the spa. I think she wanted to be sure we wouldn't interfere.

"Let's go, Megs." Ashley squealed in delight.

Two hours later, I checked myself in the tiny mirror in my cabin, feeling beautiful inside out. The steam and sauna had relaxed my aching body and soothed my mind. I wore my favorite black dress with a slash of red across my lips, my mother's signature shade. Ashley told me to step aside.

"We look hot!" she twirled around and gave me a high five.

There was a knock on the door, followed by loud rapping. Mickey and Jeong Soo stumbled in when I opened the door, looking triumphant.

"We got him, Meg!" Jeong Soo cried. "I took pictures."

I looked at Mickey for confirmation. He couldn't hold back a smile.

"He started dumping the laundry in the water. Jeong Soo captured everything on his camera."

I stole a glance at Ashley. She gave a tiny shrug but didn't look devastated which was a relief.

"What now?" I asked Mickey.

Security had whisked him away to be questioned. RK wanted to see us in her cabin. I rushed down the aisle and gave a cursory knock on her door before flinging it open.

"Come in, come in." She was grinning from ear to ear. "He just confessed, Meg. Luca Fontana admitted to being a spy for a rival cruise line."

They were still getting the complete story out of him but he had said enough. RK believed me.

"I'm sorry about the mix up, Meg. I owe you an apology."

I decided to be magnanimous and told her it was all water under the bridge. A big weight had been lifted off my shoulders. Now I just needed to figure out who killed Edmund. That was the only way to prove he hadn't taken his own life.

Chapter 24

Formal night was in full swing. Passengers were excited and most of them had chosen to dress up. Tuxedos and ball gowns were on display, along with flashy diamonds and gemstones. My mom would have fit right in and outshone everyone.

Our tour group did us proud. Max wore a simple black tux that had to be Armani or some other pricey hotshot designer. Zack's mother told me she had talked him into renting a formal jacket. Dani wore an off shoulder frock in the palest pink silk, setting off her tanned shoulders. I saw her share a secret smile with Zack. Did that mean the teen couple was on again?

Max invited us to dine with them. Anyone else would have been impressed. I wasn't. There was something about him that raised my hackles. His generosity was like a red flag. I was convinced there was something dark behind the goody goody image he projected. Might sound superstitious but I trust my sixth sense. It's helped me avoid many a sticky situation.

After feasting on more crab legs and salmon, the group was ready to stretch their legs. There was dancing in the ballroom and Cecilia told me she had given Dani and her mother dance lessons.

"I love the waltz," she confided in me, pointing at her cane. "But those days are a distant memory."

Mickey surprised me by being a very good dancer.

"Cotillion," he murmured, as he swung past me with Ashley in his arms. "You're next."

I tried to live in the moment and have a good time but the questions in my mind wouldn't let me rest. Max let us off after a couple of hours and I took the elevator down to the kitchen.

"Aren't you coming to the crew party?" Ashley asked with a pout.

Mickey and Jeong Soo each took a hand and pulled her toward the elevator. I was a bit hurt they didn't care if I went along.

I rushed to the now familiar galley and looked around for a certain face. The kitchens were a beehive of activity. I stood rooted in a spot and stared down rows and rows of cooking stations, with white coated chefs busy chopping vegetables, kneading dough and getting ready for the breakfast rush. I jumped when a hand fell on my shoulder and whirled around to come face to face with Chef Lovely. His brow was set in a frown for the first time since I'd met him.

"Not now, Meg!" He held up a hand before I could speak. "The main oven's gone cold. We may not have fresh bread for breakfast."

Hundreds of passengers looked forward to fresh croissants, Danishes and toast in the morning so the kitchen staff was really facing a big crisis. But I had a one track mind that night.

"I just need a peep at the kitchen log," I begged. "Please, Lovely. I wouldn't ask if it wasn't urgent."

He didn't crack a smile.

"Five minutes. You can check the computer in my office."

I almost hugged him again. Then I remembered how embarrassed he had been earlier and held myself back.

"Thanks! You're the best, Lovely."

I rushed toward his office before he changed his mind.

"Meg!" he called after me. "You did it. That Luca was a bad penny. We can't let him win."

My eyes widened. "The oven?"

Lovely gave a shrug but I thought his hunch was right. Luca had become more desperate as the cruise came to an end. Vandalizing the oven must have been his parting shot.

It took me a while to locate the order log for the fateful night. I ran a search for carrot cake and located the order that had been delivered to Jackie's room. Edmund's chocolate cake was next to it. But where had the order come from? Asking for Lovely's help wasn't an option so I spent some time looking around, trying to figure it out. I won't go into the intricacies of spreadsheets but I finally hit upon what I wanted. Both desserts had been ordered from the same room.

I sat back in my chair and closed my eyes, trying to process this twist. Now I needed to find out who occupied that particular cabin. My money was on Max since he had been friendly with Edmund and was prone to spread his money around. Okay, okay, he was generous and it was just the kind of thing he might do.

Somehow, I pulled up a deck plan and located the cluster of cabins occupied by the tour group. My jaw dropped open when I realized the cabin in question was located directly opposite Jackie's. The person in it had a good opportunity to tamper with Edmund's chocolate cake while the steward was in Jackie's room.

My heart thudded in my chest as I realized who the cabin belonged to.

I didn't bother to say goodbye to Chef Lovely, knowing he didn't have a second to spare. The day was finally catching up with me and I just wanted to hit the hay and get some shut eye. But Ashley was waiting for me so I made my way to the not so secret crew area where a party was raging.

The pool was full of wet bodies engrossed in swaying to some wild beats. Thousands of watts of music blared from speakers, making it impossible to think. It was exactly the relief I needed.

Ashley found me first and gave a piercing whistle. A roar went up through the crowd and everyone started clapping and cheering.

"What's happening?" I squinted my eyes, trying to

locate the source of their excitement.

"It's you, Megs." Ashley wrapped me in a tight hug. "Everyone knows what Luca was up to and they want to thank you."

She pulled out a wad of notes from her pocket and waved it in my face.

"I made a bundle because I betted on you. Most of them lost money but they don't mind. Their jobs are safe, now that Luca's in the brig."

I squeezed her arm, wondering what to say. She was putting on a brave face but she must be hurting inside.

"Don't feel sorry for me," she warned. "Good riddance."

"But …" I hesitated. "Do you feel used?"

Ashley's eyes turned cold and she pulled herself up.

"It was just a summer fling, Megs. Not worth losing sleep over."

She pulled me deeper into the crowd before I could say anything else. Before I knew it, a bunch of arms lifted me up and dunked me in the pool. I lost track of time after that.

My trusty alarm clock blared at the usual time, rousing me from the dead. I leaned over my bunk, trying to reach Ashley, mumbling to myself. I lost my balance and landed on the floor with a thud. That woke us both up.

I was half asleep even after a cold shower and dragged my feet down the I-95 to the crew mess.

"I need a gallon of coffee!" I declared, staring at the empty pot.

Jeong Soo offered to make a new one. His eyes had a gleam I hadn't seen before.

"He thinks you're a hero," Mickey scowled. "It's like you've singlehandedly warded off some disaster."

Ashley told me to ignore him. After a hearty breakfast of eggs, bacon and a stack of blueberry pancakes the kitchen staff specially sent up for me, I was ready to face the day.

There was a frenzied atmosphere across the ship. Every class and attraction was running at full capacity and the cafes and dining rooms were packed. RK told us it was always like that on the first and last day of the cruise.

"They're trying to get their money's worth," she sighed. "Squeezing every penny possible from the cruise line."

She wanted us to be extra attentive to our guests. Since the ship would not be docking anywhere, I expected our group to split up and do different activities. I was right.

Max wanted Jeong Soo to spend the day with his son at the games arcade. His wife had booked multiple treatments at the spa. Cecilia announced she was going to spend the day on the observation deck. Mickey was chosen to accompany her.

"Can I book some activity for you?" I asked Jackie. "How about a Zumba class? Or a one on one pasta making session with our Italian chef?"

"I'm just going to hang around, take it easy," she replied. "But thanks for the kind offer, Meg."

I could tell she wasn't looking forward to getting back to her job.

"You must get some time off?" I was curious. "Do

you visit your neighbors for a cup of tea or coffee?"

Jackie gave a hearty laugh.

"You think any of these people will spend time with me? I'm just the nanny. Not worth their time."

"Isn't Cecilia new to your neighborhood?" I pressed. "She must be lonely too."

Jackie rolled her eyes this time.

"That woman sits by the window with her head in a book most of the time. Poor thing! Her hip gave out just when she was getting ready to enjoy her retirement."

I commiserated with Cecilia's condition. "Doesn't look like she's in pain though."

Jackie looked over her shoulder before leaning forward.

"Drugs. I think she self-medicates."

"Are you saying she's addicted to painkillers?" My eyebrows shot up. "Opioids?"

Jackie told me Max was treating Cecilia.

"He's managed her pain pretty well." She gave me a knowing look.

Zack's mother hailed me from another table. She and her husband were lingering over their coffee, trying out an assortment of petit fours. They certainly had a sweet tooth. She pulled out a small gift bag from under the table and handed it to me.

"Just a little something for you, dear. Thank you for taking such good care of us."

I stared at her with my mouth open, unable to utter a word.

"I'm not sure I'm allowed to accept this."

"Of course you are," she dismissed. "Open it and tell me what you think."

I pulled aside a few layers of tissue to reveal a jade necklace. She must have bought it in Juneau. I'd seen strands of beads in many souvenir shops and jewelry stores.

"This looks expensive."

"It's nothing. Just promise you'll wear it sometime. I think it goes with your eyes."

I felt my eyes tear up. All the stress I'd been under for the past week vanished in an instant.

"I'm going to treasure this," I promised. "It's the perfect Alaska souvenir."

The kind couple insisted I join them for coffee. I obliged since none of the other guests needed me.

"Which excursion did you like the most?" I asked, trying to make conversation.

The train ride to Denali had been the highlight of the trip for them.

"We've been saving for this trip for a long time," she admitted. "And it was worth it."

I tried to hide my surprise but I wasn't quick enough.

"We're not all millionaires like Dr. Martin," she laughed. "Most of us work hard for a living and I think that's nothing to be ashamed of."

"Jackie works as a nanny," I mumbled. "I mean, she's a very posh nanny."

Zack's mother took pity on me.

"I think her husband left her well off. And a lot of her fancy clothes are castoffs. Why, even Cecilia Pierce had a job until she came to live with her daughter."

I held my breath, hoping she would say more. She didn't disappoint. Cecilia was a pharmacologist who had worked in drug research for several years.

"She has a patent or two in her name," Zack's mother chuckled. "Who'd have guessed that?"

Chapter 25

I roamed the decks in search of Max. He wasn't at the pub or the library. I talked to Guest Relations in the atrium and they told me about a special deck the Martin family had paid extra for. It was tucked away in a corner on Deck 4 and was a tropical paradise with lush palm trees and a riot of colorful flowers growing in big urns. Max reclined on a lounger, dark shades covering his eyes. I couldn't tell if he was awake.

I towered over him, trying to decide whether I could risk disturbing him.

"Are you done staring?" he asked a few minutes later.

"We need to talk, Max."

He sat up and pulled off the shades, his lips curling in a smirk.

"Are you in trouble, young lady?"

I didn't know what he was getting at but I assured him there was nothing wrong with me.

"It's about someone you know," I began. "One of

your patients. I need to know what you're treating her with."

"You know I can't talk about my patients." His smile was disarming. "What is it, Meg? Do you need a prescription for something? I promise this will stay between us."

"I'm fine!" I tried to control my frustration. "Is Cecilia Pierce your patient?"

His smile didn't waver but I could see his eyes narrow.

"What if she is? So is almost everyone in the tour group. It's very convenient for them since we're neighbors."

"Her hip's in bad condition but she doesn't seem to be in pain. That means you're managing it well."

Max leaned back in his chair and stared over the water, putting his arms around his head. The sunshine was bright and there was only a slight nip in the air.

"How many pills is she taking?" I blustered. "Enough to make her erratic?"

He told me our conversation was over. But I wasn't done.

"You must've noticed how unpredictable she is? Sometimes she's sweet as sugar but she flares up when you least expect it. Drugs can have side effects like that."

I couldn't force a response out of him. Max asked me to book a table at the Japanese restaurant for lunch. It was his way of dismissing me, of course.

I stalked off, trying to figure out my next move. Dani materialized from behind a potted palm and placed a finger on her lips. I followed her and we took the stairs to go one floor up to a small café. She insisted I sit and came back with two cappuccinos and a big brownie.

"I saw you talking to my Dad."

I had no idea where this was going so I didn't interrupt.

"Cecilia's crazy. I mean, she's mentally ill."

That got my attention alright. Dani told me she had overheard Max talking to Cecilia's daughter.

"She's paranoid, you know. Dad said she was getting worse and time was running out."

Poor Cecilia! She was a victim, just like Edmund. Max Martin had manipulated two weak patients and committed the perfect crime. No wonder he thought he got away with it.

I tried to maintain a poker face before Dani. She might not be so friendly if she knew I was planning to accuse her Dad of murder.

"Are you sure about this?" I cut the brownie in half and took a big bite. "You could've been mistaken."

"I'm sure, Meg. She's a crackpot. I've seen her walk around the block at 2 AM in the morning."

I wanted to ask Dani why she wasn't tucked into her bed at that hour. Probably out canoodling with Zack or Edmund but I wasn't her parent so I said nothing.

"You ready to go home?" I was curious. "Any plans for the summer?"

Dani told me she was going to volunteer at a local clinic. I was impressed and I told her so, eliciting a smile. Luckily, she didn't ask me what I was going to do about Cecilia.

We parted ways at the atrium and I went in search of my boss. One of the stewards told me she was doing paperwork in her office. I knocked on the now familiar door and went in. For the first time since I'd boarded the Silver Queen, RK greeted me with a smile.

"Well, Meg? I hear the crew gave you quite a reception last night."

She knew about the crew party?

"I was young once," RK sighed. "And I worked my way up from housekeeping."

I was dumbstruck. Did she also know about the betting pool? She didn't look like she'd lost a bundle.

"Max Martin killed Edmund," I blurted out.

RK's smile froze.

"What is this nonsense, girl? Why don't you quit while you're ahead?"

I poured out the whole story. Only, I did it in a random sequence so all that came out was gibberish.

"You're not making sense." RK told me to sit and

offered me a bottle of water. "Now begin at the beginning."

I gathered my thoughts while I took a sip of water and tried to be more coherent this time. I must have succeeded a bit because the boss didn't shoot me down immediately.

"Max Martin told us Edmund's heart gave out. Who's going to challenge a doctor's word?"

"Exactly!" I spread my arms wide. "And does he show an ounce of remorse? He thinks he got away with it."

RK told me Edmund Toole's death would be reported to the authorities when the ship docked in port. She would talk to the captain and tell him that foul play was suspected.

"I have a better plan."

I never do anything halfheartedly. So I took the plunge and tried to get her to agree.

"I'll have extra security on hand," she nodded. "But be very careful, Meg. I'm doing this against my better judgment."

I told her she was doing the right thing.

The crew mess was my next stop. Ashley was there with Mickey and Jeong Soo, having a late lunch. Her eyes popped out when I outlined what I was thinking.

"You're wrong about Dr. Martin," Jeong Soo cried. "He received the Humanitarian of the Year award from the medical council. You know how many lives he saved during the California wildfires?"

"Yeah, yeah." I rolled my eyes. "I trust my instincts. Max Martin is no Mother Teresa."

Mickey clapped his hands and laughed.

"You're such a hoot, Meg Butler. Do you think you're Hercule Poirot?"

I ignored him and went to the buffet, loading a plate with a cheesy chicken and rice casserole and green salad. Battles are not won on an empty stomach.

We spent the afternoon scurrying around, helping our tour group play a game of trivia, take pilates, salsa dancing and origami classes, ride the aqua roller coaster, get their hair done and a dozen other things. They also managed a high tea along with everything else.

"Don't spoil your appetite," Max warned his family. "We're having dinner at the Steakhouse tonight." He summoned us closer and blessed us with his gracious smile. "You're all invited, of course. I already talked to your boss."

Ashley and I primped before the tiny mirror in our cabin that evening. I'd worn my black frock many times so she lent me a green sequined top to wear with my black harem pants. I was ready to go beard the lion in his den.

Max had ensured he got the best table. It was in the center of the restaurant on a slightly raised platform. Champagne was chilling on ice and an assortment of Hors d'oeuvres had been laid out.

I popped a goat cheese tart in my mouth and said hello to Jackie. The waiter opened the champagne with some fanfare and began pouring.

"What shall we drink to?" Max beamed. "Alaska?"

"More trips together," Ruth added.

It was now or never.

"How about Edmund?" I stared into Max's eyes. "He was your dear friend, wasn't he?"

Max frowned for a split second but recovered quickly.

"Of course! In loving memory of Edmund. May he rest in peace."

"People who die violent deaths seldom do," I ventured. "Unless you're going to confess you murdered him."

There was a stunned silence around the table. Tori Martin was the first to speak up.

"How dare you! Get out of here, you piece of trash."

Max was looking amused.

"Do you have any proof, Meg?"

I shook my head.

"You took care of that, I guess. I don't know what kind of drugs you used to kill the poor man, but I'm willing to bet they won't find anything in the autopsy."

RK was standing in a dark corner, flanked by two beefy security guards. She gave a slight nod, prodding me on. I sensed some of the people seated at the adjoining tables were also part of the ship's staff.

"Why have I done this heinous act?" Max smiled but his eyes were cold this time. "Surely I must have a motive."

I stole a quick glance at Dani before surging ahead.

"You thought he was misbehaving with your daughter."

"What?" Max burst out, turning toward his daughter. "That rascal! Is that right, Dani?"

"Of course not, Dad!" Dani flashed me a look full of venom. "He was helping me with math."

"Did you know about this?" Max turned on his wife.

She told him to calm down and get rid of me. That seemed to rally him.

"So let me get this straight, Meg. I killed Edmund and declared his death was from a heart attack. What else? How did I do this, huh?"

This is where things got a bit fuzzy. I hadn't been completely straight with RK so I hoped she would still have my back after this.

"You framed Cecilia," I shot back. "She was your stooge, Max, ready to take the fall in case things got hot."

All eyes in the room were on me, making me squirm in my chair.

"The poor woman is ill. You fed her some drugs and manipulated her, Max. I'm not sure how."

Mickey was looking at me, slowly shaking his head. Was he urging me to stick to my guns or feeling sorry for me? It was anybody's guess.

Max waved a hand in the air and pointed at his empty glass. A waiter sprang forward to top it up with more champagne.

"You're shooting blanks, kid." He laughed until there were tears in his eyes. "Better luck next time."

RK came out of her dark corner and greeted everyone loudly. She hoped they were having a good time.

"Is this how you train your employees?" Tori Martin complained. "I'm telling all my friends."

RK's face turned red and she hastened to apologize.

"Champagne on the house," she giggled nervously. "It's actually a pilot for dinner theater. We wanted to get your unbiased reactions."

"The chit's not completely wrong." Cecilia Pierce tapped her cane. "Megan's right about one thing. I poisoned that twerp Edmund. He got off easy, if you ask me."

Max shot up from his chair and hurried to Cecilia. RK gave some hidden signal and the security guys surrounded our table.

"Have you taken your pills today, my dear?" Max asked, keeping a firm hand on her shoulder. "Why don't you turn in early tonight?"

Cecilia shook him off.

"That's enough, Doc! Edmund Toole was an enemy of the state. Didn't I tell you so? But would you listen?"

"It was the cake, wasn't it?" I leaned forward in my

chair. "You poisoned the chocolate cake when the server was in Jackie's room."

Cecilia gave a shrug.

"He left me no choice. It was either him or me. I warned him, you know."

She had been spying on Edmund for a long time, sure he was up to no good. He went for walks in the middle of the night and a bunch of shady people visited him at odd hours. She was afraid for her life so she had come prepared. That night, she ordered dessert from room service and poured cyanide over the chocolate cake meant for Edmund.

I felt a chill run up my spine. I was so out of depth here. RK took over. Max convinced Cecilia to go with the security staff. Dinner was forgotten as all eyes turned to Max.

"What?" he cried. "She's my patient. I was trying to protect her. And that's all I'm going to say. Any details about her condition and treatment are confidential."

Something wasn't adding up.

"That doesn't explain why you tried to cover up

Edmund's murder. He was your patient too."

Max stalked off without gracing me with a reply. Dani looked stricken. Tori Martin offered her theory.

"What good would that have done? I think he was protecting Edmund."

Dani sprang up and glared at her stepmother.

"He was just being selfish, Tori. My guess is he didn't want anything to disturb his vacation. The perfect family vacation, right?"

I believed there was more to it.

Zack's parents were in shock. His mother finally pulled herself together and told us they were leaving. RK promised to send dinner to their cabins.

Jackie had been plowing through the champagne, getting quite drunk.

"That old bat!" Her laugh was hysterical. "Always thought she had a screw loose." She tapped the side of her head. "Edmund was no saint though."

In vino veritas, right? Was Jackie about to reveal more secrets?

"I think he was dealing on the side," she whispered, banging the empty champagne bottle on the table.

"You mean drugs?" My mouth dropped open.

I hadn't seen this coming.

"Pills." Jackie gave a slight shrug. "Cecilia was right about one thing. He acted very hush hush because he was doing something illegal."

Tori Martin dropped her glass. All eyes turned to her as it crashed on the wood floor, shattering into a hundred pieces. Her face began to turn red.

"Let's go, Dani." She gathered her kids together. "We've heard enough."

"You think Jackie's lying?" I was curious.

Tori Martin ignored me and propelled her kids out of the room. I had a crazy thought. Had Max been hand in glove with Edmund? It would have been so easy for him to write fake prescriptions and procure drugs. As his patient, Edmund had reason to see him officially and was the perfect conduit. That could have been why Dr. Max Martin did not want to draw attention to Edmund's death. Any investigation in his life would put the doctor at risk.

All these speculations flew out of my head when I felt myself grabbed from both sides. Mickey and Ashley almost dragged me out of the restaurant with Jeong Soo close behind. Ashley brandished a bottle of champagne in one hand.

"You did it, Megs," she crowed. "You solved that guy's murder."

I didn't realize where they were taking me until we stepped out in the open on Deck 2. We were near the bow of the Silver Queen. The area was deserted with signs warning that it was a restricted zone.

"Are we allowed to be here?" I gazed at the flaming sky and the roiling ocean below us. "What if RK needs us?"

Mickey popped the cork on the champagne bottle and offered it to me. His warm brown eyes spoke volumes.

"Welcome aboard, Meg!"

Epilogue

Three months later

The sun shone on a group of people gathered at the stern on the Lido Deck. The captain was flanked by his first officer on the right and RK on the left. Four interns stood before him, looking proud. A bunch of people sat on chairs, there by special invitation.

I couldn't believe I was actually going to meet the captain of the Silver Queen. After a stormy start, three months had just flown. I had been exposed to many different jobs as the ship made multiple trips to Alaska. Between the rigorous work days, late night parties and shore trips, I had somehow managed to sample almost every dish that came out of the kitchen and squeeze in a few hours of sleep. Mickey had been true to his word and had played fair, holding off on any more pranks. The day we'd been waiting for had finally arrived. The captain was going to announce the winner of the internship prize.

RK cleared her throat and congratulated us on successfully completing the program. I held my breath as she handed an envelope to the captain. He pulled out a slip of paper and squinted his eyes, making a show of reading it.

"Meg Butler," he announced with a broad smile. "And Mickey Singh."

It was a tie. I turned to my right and offered my hand to Mickey. He took it and pulled me into a hug. Ashley and Jeong Soo joined in.

Mom and Grandma were clapping with abandon, so were Mickey's parents.

RK had arranged a celebratory brunch for our group. Ashley was the only one who didn't have a family member present but Grandma had taken an instant liking to her. I had no doubt she would take my new friend under her wing. Jeong Soo's parents were bright eyed, having a fan moment with my mom.

Edmund Toole's autopsy hadn't yielded much but the police had arrested Cecilia based on her confession. An investigation into Edmund's life confirmed that he had been illegally supplying prescription drugs. Max Martin was the one who had talked him into it. Although he had not been involved in Edmund's murder, he had played a part by declaring he died a natural death. His license to practise medicine had been suspended and he would probably go to prison for procuring drugs based on fake prescriptions.

RK tapped a spoon on her mimosa glass to get everyone's attention.

"Congratulations everyone! You did an excellent job this summer." She took a sip and beamed around the table. "Mickey and Meg, as winners of the internship prize, you are supposed to get a job offer with the cruise line."

There was a lot of cheering and back slapping. I could tell Ashley was trying to put on a brave face. She really needed this job and had worked harder than anyone to get it.

"Actually, all four of you have gone above and beyond," RK continued. "So I'm pleased to offer a job to each and every one of you."

"What?" Ashley cried. "For reals?"

RK made a show of rolling her eyes.

"Yes, Ashley, I'm serious."

The meal began with grilled oyster salad and soup. A platter of Alaskan King Crab followed, along with fried cod and salmon cooked three different ways. RK wasn't skimping on giving us a grand farewell.

"Are you sure you won't accept the job?" Mickey asked me.

My grandma had a smile on her face but my mom looked tense. She had dropped out of high school to try her luck in Hollywood. A college degree meant a lot to my family and I wasn't going to disappoint them.

"It's back to school for the next two years," I replied. "That was always the plan."

"And after that?" he held my gaze.

"After that? Que Sera Sera …" I sipped my mimosa, laughing as the bubbles tickled my nose. "But I'm going to visit thirty countries before I'm thirty."

**

What's next for Meg? Will she finish college or take up the new job? Get your copy of Bingo Bashed and find out.

https://www.amazon.com/dp/B0BZKK6FWX

Acknowledgements

I enjoyed writing Croissants and Cruises so much, I made up my mind to create a new series dedicated to cruising. Meg was the perfect candidate for it because she had a penchant for adventure and was eager to spread her wings. But any new project comes with its own set of challenges, right from deciding on the titles to creating the characters. I am thankful for all the people who lent a hand in bringing you this book and series.

Thank you to all my readers who eagerly read every new title I present and support my author journey. I really appreciate you and am happy to have you here.

My beta readers and reviewers deserve a special mention since they spot errors early on and help me put forward a better version of the book.

As always, my family has my eternal gratitude for being with me every step of the way and holding my hand through the vagaries of life.

Thank you to all of you who comment on social media, message or email me, encouraging me to write more. I appreciate it.

Thank you for reading this book. If you enjoyed this book, please consider leaving a brief review. Even a few words or a line or two will do.

As an indie author, I rely on reviews to spread the word about my book. Your assistance will be very helpful and greatly appreciated.

I would also really appreciate it if you tell your friends and family about the book. Word of mouth is an author's best friend, and it will be of immense help to me.

Many Thanks!

Author Leena Clover

http://leenaclover.com

Leenaclover@gmail.com

https://www.facebook.com/leenaclovercozymysterybooks

Other books by Leena Clover

Pelican Cove Cozy Mystery Series -

Strawberries and Strangers

Cupcakes and Celebrities

Berries and Birthdays

Sprinkles and Skeletons

Waffles and Weekends

Muffins and Mobsters

Truffles and Troubadours

Sundaes and Sinners

Croissants and Cruises

Pancakes and Parrots

Cookies and Christmas

Popsicles and Poisons

Biscuits and Butlers

Dolphin Bay Cozy Mystery Series

Raspberry Chocolate Murder

Orange Thyme Death

Apple Caramel Mayhem

Cranberry Sage Miracle

Blueberry Chai Frenzy

Mango Chili Cruiser

Strawberry Vanilla Peril

Cherry Lime Havoc

Pumpkin Ginger Bedlam

Meera Patel Cozy Mystery Series -

Gone with the Wings

A Pocket Full of Pie

For a Few Dumplings More

Back to the Fajitas

British Cozy Mystery Series

Murder at Buxley Manor

Murder at Castle Morse

Murder at Ridley Hall

Join my Newsletter

Get access to exclusive bonus content, sneak peeks, giveaways and much more. Also get a chance to join my exclusive ARC group, the people who get first dibs on all my new books.

Sign up at the following link and join the fun.

Visit here →
http://www.subscribepage.com/leenaclovernl

I love to hear from my readers, so please feel free to connect with me at any of the following places.

Website – http://leenaclover.com

Facebook –
http://facebook.com/leenaclovercozymysterybo oks

Instagram – http://instagram.com/leenaclover

Email – leenaclover@gmail.com

Printed in Great Britain
by Amazon

57421247R00175